PRAISE FOR
CAROL HIGGINS CLARK AND
SNAGGED

♦ ♦ ♦

"Hilarious . . . Sleuth Regan Reilly wraps everything up neatly in the heartwarming tale."
—***Denver Rocky Mountain News***

♦

"Upbeat, fast-paced."
—***New York Times Book Review***

♦

"A bit of bawdy, a soupçon of slapstick . . . no one can read just one page."
—***Washington Post***

♦

"Should delight fans of whimsical whodunits."
—***Baltimore Sun***

♦

"Breezy and humorous . . . *Snagged* offers a run on fun and enter
—***Fort La***

D1016406

"Fresh and funny, *Snagged* keeps you thoroughly entertained."
—West Coast Review of Books

◆

"A superb mystery writer."
—Washington Times

◆

"Carol Higgins Clark tells a fast-paced, suspenseful story, with never a dull moment and a refreshing sense of humor."
—Mostly Murder

◆

"Carol Higgins Clark has created some delightful characters—highly individualistic, yet down to earth—who frolic through her well-crafted stories, creating humor and satisfying reading in the midst of mystery and mayhem."
—Chattanooga Times

◆

"Such fun . . . Clark writes with skill and humor . . . there's much to like in this tale."
—Miami Herald

BOOKS BY CAROL HIGGINS CLARK

Decked

Snagged

Iced

Twanged

Fleeced

Jinxed

Popped

Burned

Hitched

Laced

Deck the Halls
(with Mary Higgins Clark)

He Sees You When You're Sleeping
(with Mary Higgins Clark)

The Christmas Thief
(with Mary Higgins Clark)

Santa Cruise (with Mary Higgins Clark)

CAROL HIGGINS CLARK

SNAGGED

GRAND CENTRAL
PUBLISHING

NEW YORK   BOSTON

Copyright © 1993 by Carol Higgins Clark
All rights reserved. Except as permitted under the U.S. Copyright Act of 1976, no part of this publication may be reproduced, distributed, or transmitted in any form or by any means, or stored in a database or retrieval system, without the prior written permission of the publisher.

Grand Central Publishing
Hachette Book Group USA
237 Park Avenue
New York, NY 10017
Visit our Web site at www.HachetteBookGroupUSA.com

Grand Central Publishing is a division of Hachette Book Group USA, Inc.
The Grand Central Publishing name and logo is a trademark of Hachette Book Group USA, Inc.

Printed in the United States of America

Originally published in hardcover by Hachette Book Group USA
First Paperback Edition: August 1994
First Special Price Edition: May 2008

10   9   8   7   6   5   4   3   2

For my siblings and sibling-in-law,
Marilyn, Warren and Sharon, David, and Patty,
with love.

Regan Reilly would like to thank the following people for assisting in her birth: Michael Viner, Nanscy Neiman, Larry Kirshbaum, Maureen Mahon Egen, Eugene Winick, and Lisl Cade. She is also grateful to the author's mother, Mary Higgins Clark, for introducing her daughter to a life of crime!

Snag—any obstacle or impediment

Ride on! Rough-shod if need be, smooth-shod if that
will do, but ride on! Ride on over all obstacles,
and win the race!

Charles Dickens

RICHIE BLOSSOM TUMBLED from the side of his bed as he bent over in an awkward attempt to pull on his brand-new pair of panty hose. "Birdie," he exclaimed, smacking a kiss in the direction of the enlarged Kodak of his late wife, snapped at their last picnic in the backyard, "I wish you were the one wiggling into these." His writhing contortions matted down the flecked, gold-and-sea-green shag rug that had been bought in celebration of their forty-fifth wedding anniversary.

"Yahoo," he yelled to his reflection in the mirror on the closet door as he kicked his heels in the air, "even the nails of the Wicked Witch couldn't put a run in these babies." Like a June Taylor dancer, he splayed his legs, then brought them together, practicing the scissor motion that had become so popular in aerobics classes, as he admired his satiny gams. "Not a run, not even a snag," he muttered enthusiastically. He grabbed the material around his right foot and pulled hard, knowing that the callus on his heel would normally be rough enough to split wood. He let go of the luxurious fabric bunched in his hand, started to sit up, and then, for good measure, gave it one more yank before bending his leg and pulling it close for further examination. "There isn't a mark," he whispered.

He looked around anxiously, as though someone could hear him. The run-proof, snag-proof, callus-proof panty hose was his invention. The realization of the dream he had had when Birdie, short for Bird Legs, had never been able to find hose that didn't blow in the wind around her matchstick ankles. She had tugged and yanked at them so much that no pair ever lasted more than one round of miniature golf.

"Birdie, Birdie, Birdie," he sighed happily, gazing at the picture that unfortunately had been clicked just as Birdie was about to yell at him to hurry up. It was the last picture on the roll, so no retake had been possible. Birdie's unexpected demise in her sleep that night meant that Kodak was out a sale and her panty-hose troubles were laid to rest. "But I've created this masterpiece in your memory, my little buttercup. Women will be able to buy it in any color, and each pair will last for years. Who in the world could have any objection to that?''

Maybe it was the way the sun slanted through the thick Miami air and reflected off Birdie's scrunched-up nose in the picture frame, but one thing was for sure. Birdie looked worried.

THE ROAR AND vibrations of the 747's engines underneath Regan Reilly's feet were no match for the snap, crackle and popping of her neighbor's gum. For hours she had tried to ignore it as they crossed the country, but the wad of Bazooka in her seatmate's mouth was continually being replaced with the next stick in an economy pack. The only respite was during the doll-sized "meal," which Regan picked at before abandoning the miniature fork, deciding that the dollop on her tray, grandly termed lasagna al forno, bore an uncomfortable resemblance to mystery meals she had endured in college.

Regan pushed the button to ease her seat back, hearing the annoyed sigh of the person sitting behind her, and closed her eyes. She bolted upright seconds later when the first bubble from a fresh piece of gum was enthusiastically decimated by her seatmate, who was now buried in a tabloid whose headline warned of UFOs bearing pregnant skeletons landing at Euro Disney. Where's Miss Manners when you need her? Regan thought. Probably riding in first class.

Feeling her body twitch as another bubble lost its fight for survival, Regan leaned forward and pulled her copy of *USA Today* out of the seat pocket in front of her. For some reason she always loved to read this newspaper on airplanes, checking out the weather map for the conditions of the cities all over the country, and especially the ones they were passing thirty thousand feet below. Not exactly like traveling in a wagon train, with the wind blowing off your bonnet, but with a little imagination one could conjure up a nasty day in Butte, Montana, or dismal skies, not too promising, in Chicago. But one thing Regan could never understand was why the captain would get hold of the microphone and interrupt the in-flight movie to announce that the speck below was the Grand Canyon. Oh, great. Let's all raise our window shades and make the actors on the screen a bunch of shadows and the people who paid their four bucks for the headsets a bunch of squinters yelling, "Pull down the shades!"

Once again Regan read the prediction for her destination—Miami, Florida. Muggy and hot. No surprise there. Regan, who had inherited the pale skin, blue eyes and dark hair of her Irish forebears, was not a sun worshiper, but she loved a swim in the ocean.

A thirty-year-old private investigator from Los

Angeles, Regan Reilly was coming to Miami to be a bridesmaid for the ninth time. This occasion was the nuptials of her childhood friend Maura Durkin. Maura's father, Ed, had worked for Regan's father, Luke, in his first funeral home in Summit, New Jersey, then decided to open his own place in Miami, where business was always good. The families had remained close and Regan's parents and Maura's parents always saw each other at the annual funeral convention, which, not so coincidentally, was being held in Miami this weekend.

"You know old Ed," Maura had told Regan. "He wants all his friends from the biz at the wedding, and what better time to schedule it than when they're all going to be down here anyway. Besides," she added, "I think he's getting a break on the flowers from a floral exhibitor at the convention."

"I imagine there are a few sample guest books floating around you could grab too," Regan replied, "not to mention limousines, cosmetologists who can do your makeup, hair . . ."

"Oh, I already asked the woman who does the hair for my father's clients if she'd be interested, but she says she has no experience doing the backs of people's heads."

"OH, GOD!" Regan had always laughed with her oldest friend at some of the absurdities of growing up with a mortician father, a bond they would share until death did them part. When they were little and discovered "The Munsters" television show, where Herman, the father, worked at a funeral parlor, Regan and Maura had gone through a stage where they called their fathers

Hermie. But their parents drew the line when the girls wanted to make telephone booths out of upright coffins.

"Ladies and gentlemen, please bring your seat backs to their upright and locked positions, stow away your tray tables, and make sure your seat belts are securely fastened. We'll be landing at Miami International Airport in a few minutes."

There is a God, Regan thought as she obediently complied, making sure that her carry-on bag, which weighed at least a ton, was completely tucked under the seat in front of her. If that thing went flying, Regan thought, someone would end up with whiplash. But if it could just be used to dislodge gum . . .

The plane swayed from side to side and finally landed with a thump, streamlining down the runway. Scattered applause and a wolf call from a college kid who'd enjoyed a few beers along the way resounded in the aircraft. With her long red fingernails, the bone-thin woman next to Regan, who Regan figured was probably in her early thirties, daintily plucked the pale-pink gob from her mouth, wrapped it in a tissue and proceeded to re-ruby her lips, powder her nose, and smilingly spritz herself with Jardin de Roses perfume that two seconds later assaulted the olfactory glands of everyone in a three-row radius.

"My boyfriend is picking me up," she said with a smile to Regan. "He hates it when I chew gum."

"Oh, really." Regan made an attempt at a laugh that to her ears came out sounding incredibly fake.

"Yeah, but I get so nervous on planes, it makes me feel better. It also helps your ears pop, you know." She fluffed her light-brown hair as she once again glanced at her pretty but tough face in the mirror of her compact. "My boyfriend has a really good job in real estate down here. So I'm gonna lay on the beach while he works. I can't wait."

"Sounds great."

"Ladies and gentlemen, welcome to Miami International Airport. Please remain seated until the aircraft has come to a complete halt and the captain has turned off the seat-belt sign . . ."

Before the announcement was finished, the clicks of unfastening seat belts echoed up and down the aisles of the 747 as impatient passengers shifted in their seats and began to gather their belongings.

"Sir, please remain seated until the aircraft has come to a complete halt," the flight attendant chirped in a cheerful but firm tone to a traveler already fumbling for his carry-on bag from the overhead compartment. "Federal regulations require that you remain seated—"

"All right, all right," the stout middle-aged man grunted as he snapped the compartment shut, his bowling bag now secure under his arm. As he reclaimed his seat, Regan gazed out the window at the hot tarmac, which from a distance looked as if it were hosting a jellyfish hootenanny. Squiggles moving up and down and bouncing back and forth similar to the kind you see right before you faint, Regan thought. It must be hot out there. A late-day swim and a jog on the beach sound pretty good to me. After sitting for over five hours, she was anxious to move and stretch.

Regan had a reservation at a hotel on Ocean Drive in the South Beach area of Miami, a section that had been renovated in the past five years and transformed into a pastel Art Deco wonderland, complete with trendy restaurants, hotels and sidewalk cafés right across from the beach, and great for people-watching. Modeling agencies had recently sprung up, as fashion photographers started to take advantage of the beautiful setting and weather.

Luke and Nora were staying a few miles away at the Watergreen, which would be filled with morticians who would be ready to boogie on Sunday afternoon in the Grand Ballroom.

"All the rooms at the Watergreen have been booked for over a year," Maura had said.

"Are there that many morticians descending on Miami this weekend?" Regan had asked incredulously.

"No, but get this. There's also a panty-hose convention coming to town."

"It sounds like a weekend to load up on free samples."

"Control top, thank you. Anyway, I made you a reservation at a hotel in South Beach. It's funky and more fun anyway. It's a few doors down from where my Uncle Richie lives—"

"How is he?" Regan interrupted. "Has he invented anything new lately? Those chunky earrings he sent me that held a 'big surprise' sure did. They started tinkling 'You Light Up My Life' when I was out on a date. Needless to say, I never heard from the guy again."

"He gave me the same pair. Luckily I was already

engaged. Anyway, now Uncle Richie says he's really outdone himself, inventing a run-proof, snag-proof panty hose.''

"If he did, it would be the Eighth Wonder of the World.''

"No kidding. Right now he's in the process of letting all the big hosiery companies know about it. I think he wants to start a bidding war.''

"Well, if they really are unsnaggable, I'm sure the big panty-hose companies will be after them in one way or another. The last thing they want on the market is panty hose that will last more than thirty seconds.''

"You're right, Regan. And right now he's also trying to save the Fourth Quarter, that's the old folks' place where he lives, from being bought out. He moved there after Aunt Birdie died. They all have their own apartments, but there's a community room where they socialize. Richie needs a lot of money by Monday, when their option on the place expires. That real estate on Ocean Drive has gotten really valuable. Naturally there's a lot of people who want to get in on it, but that means squeezing out the older people who've been there forever but can't keep up with the higher taxes. So with his new invention and the panty-hose people being around this weekend, God knows what he'll be up to.''

Regan waited until the plane emptied before getting up, preferring the seated position to the hunched-over variety that people were forced into while waiting for the people jamming the aisles to start filing out.

Everyone in a rush to go stand around the baggage-claim area. Regan's seatmate had said a hurried "Have

a nice time," as she charged up the aisle on what Regan
assumed were the wings of love. I guess if you have a
hot date meeting you, Regan thought, there is more of
an incentive to cut people off on your way out. But
when the next person you'll end up conversing with is
most likely a taxi driver in a bad mood, what's the
hurry?

Down at the baggage carousel Regan stood for a good
eight minutes before a buzzer went off and a red light
started flashing, an oddly celebratory way to announce
the slow arrival of everyone's goodies. The conveyor
started to move and Regan watched as one suitcase after
another was spit out of the chute, slid down the ramp
before crashing into the wall, and silently rode on as
each piece waited to be claimed, sometimes being
chased by an owner not fast enough to grab it before it
disappeared around the bend.

Regan shifted impatiently as baby seats, cardboard
boxes, and suitcases tied together with twine, masking
tape, and what Regan assumed was a prayer, all made
an entrance. After what seemed like an eternity, her big
blue-gray suitcase finally showed up. Regan broke into
a big smile and realized that she must have looked as if
she were greeting a lover as she lunged forward, throwing her arms around it, pulling it close to get it off the
conveyor belt and over the hump. That accomplished,
she swiftly retrieved her garment bag with one arm and
wheeled her suitcase toward the exit with the other.
Wheels on the bottom of suitcases were a great invention, Regan thought, except when they behave like the
wheels on your average shopping cart, stopping dead or

locking themselves in a position where the only thing they will do is make a never-ending right turn. Regan sometimes wondered if she'd ever get a decent shopping cart on the first yank from the bunch corralled together in the entrance to her local supermarket.

Outside the terminal the Miami air was hot and sticky. Regan felt her energy drain and longed to be in her hotel room already, relaxing with a cool drink. As her suitcase squeaked, she made her way over to the taxi stand and was surprised to find her seatmate at the head of the long line. Where's lover boy? Regan thought.

Their eyes met. Her fellow passenger shouted, "I'm going to the South Beach area. Where are you headed?"

"South Beach," Regan yelled back as the people in front of her glared.

"Wanna ride together?"

Regan debated fiercely. Did she want to share a cab? They hadn't even talked much on the plane. But the line was long.

"My boyfriend's paying."

That does it, Regan thought, and stumbling over the litter of suitcases on the sidewalk, hurried to the waiting cab.

As the driver piled the luggage in the trunk, Regan listened in awe to the instructions he was receiving.

"Put the blue one on the bottom. Don't crush the green one, it's got all my toiletries. Lay the garment bag on top. Don't get it too near that greasy tire. You know, if you're gonna be picking people up at the airport, you really should clean out your trunk."

The scrawny leather-skinned driver reminded Regan

of Popeye. Regan thought she saw him push the garment bag toward the offensive tire the instant before he slammed the trunk shut.

The luggage director, her voice sounding satisfied, said, "Okey-doke. Let's get on our way." She turned to Regan and extended her hand. "Hi. I'm Nadine Berry."

"Regan Reilly. This is really nice of you. That line doesn't look like it's moving too fast."

"That's because we're holding it up," the cabbie snarled. "Get in."

The interior of the cab offered an unlovely combination of dried perspiration and smoke, which was made worse by the Christmas-tree-shaped air freshener dangling from the mirror.

"Turn on the air conditioner," Nadine ordered.

"It's broken," the driver said as the car lurched forward and a lit cigarette magically appeared between his lips.

"Put that out," Nadine commanded, "or we'll have to take a different cab."

"I should be so lucky," the Popeye look-alike muttered as he squashed the butt in the ashtray.

Nadine turned to Regan. "If there's anything I can't stand, it's cigarette smoke. A terrible habit." She opened her bag and pulled out her gum. "Want some?"

"No, thanks. I thought your boyfriend was picking you up."

"He couldn't. You know how I told you he works in a real estate office. There's a meeting of the big shots at five-thirty and they made him stay to answer the phones. Where are you staying anyhow?"

"The Ocean View on Ocean Drive."

"Oh, that's right near the old folks' home!" Nadine exclaimed and then lowered her voice. "Everyone at Joey's office is sitting on pins and needles. An option expires on that home Monday, and there's a lot of money at stake."

Oh, brother, Regan thought. That's got to be Richie's place. The poor guy.

It took forty minutes to get to the Ocean View. By the time they arrived, Regan had heard Nadine's autobiography. Nadine was twenty-seven, sold stereos in a discount store outside of Los Angeles, and had met Joey at a Club Med vacation in Hawaii. She had been jetting back and forth to visit him for nearly six months. "He pays for every other trip," she confided. "It's easier for me to come here because he's been working so much on weekends."

As the cab neared the Ocean View, Nadine said, "What about you?"

Regan had to make it quick. "I live in Los Angeles. I'm here to be in a friend's wedding this weekend."

"Oh, I've been a bridesmaid so many times. All those dresses you never wear again, but every time they promise you'll get a lot of use out of them. I say yeah, sure, on Halloween. By the way, what do you do?"

"I'm a private investigator."

Nadine's eyes and mouth became perfect circles. "That sounds really interesting. Do you pack a gun?"

"I'm licensed to carry one but I never bring it on a trip like this."

"Do you ever get in real danger?"

"Sometimes," Regan laughed.

"Listen, Joey's apartment is only a few blocks from here. I'll be on the beach when he's at work. Maybe we can get together if you have any free time."

"Great," Regan said with a heartiness she hoped didn't sound forced. "Can't I help you pay for this?"

Nadine waved her hand. "Not at all. Joey's the greatest. Once I set foot in Miami, he tells me to put away my wallet."

The cab stopped in front of a pale-purple hotel with an outdoor café. In a few minutes I'll be in air-conditioning and drinking something cold, Regan thought.

BARNEY FREIZE WAITED nervously in the plush reception room of the Calla-Lily Hosiery Company. Across the wall a poster-sized edition of the ad that had appeared in all the fashion magazines showed a pair of exquisite legs clad in shimmering black panty hose. The copy began: "The Calla-Lily legs are in bloom again."

Freize knew that Calla-Lily hosiery enjoyed the position of being the number-one choice of well-shod women in America and abroad. Those women didn't mind paying through the nose to have their legs look good.

Barney studied the ad. "The Birdie stockings look better than them," he muttered. He pulled up his own socks and brushed the lint off his Hush Puppies. "Yup, if I were a dame, I'd be happy to get my hands on a pair of the Birdie specials.'' He looked up quickly. I've got to stop talking to myself out loud, he thought. They'll have me committed just like they did Cousin Vince. Now there was one crazy cat.

The Muzak piped in from a seemingly invisible speaker started to play "Luck, Be a Lady Tonight." Barney found himelf humming. Talk about luck, he thought. Whatever possessed him to take a walk past the old panty-hose factory that night he didn't know. He'd worked there in the maintenance department for years, until nine months ago, when they finally had to shut the place down. Business wasn't good enough. The owners never realized that specializing in panty hose for clerics just might be a slightly outdated idea. And now the place was going to be demolished.

But in the meantime his fellow maintenance worker Richie Blossom had been hanging around the place, setting up a little research lab, tinkering with the machines, up to his usual business of trying to invent something useless. But when Barney peered in the window that night and watched Richie fiddling with scraps of fabric, he just got a feeling that this time it might be different.

Barney's curiosity was piqued. He knew that if he knocked on the door, Richie wouldn't tell him what he was doing. So he went home and searched through all his maintenance uniforms, which he sentimentally kept heaped in the corner of his closet, and found what he hoped might be there. A key to the side door of the panty-hose factory.

The next night he waited outside until Richie had

left, gave him fifteen minutes in case he had forgotten something, then let himself in. Armed with his flashlight, he started looking around.

The old picnic table where they had gulped their coffee during their strictly observed five-minute breaks hadn't been moved; Richie was obviously using it as the command station for his project. Barney couldn't count the number of times he'd ended up with a burned tongue as he rushed to swallow the black brew that was passed off as coffee.

The gray time clock attached to the wall was still there, clicking away. Barney went over and gave it a punch, remembering all the misery it had brought him. "There," he smirked. "I didn't forget to punch in."

Stacks of cheap paper with a printed message, the kind that people force on you when you're running down the block late for an appointment, were lined up on the table. Barney picked one up, and with the glow of his flashlight began to read Richie's literature on his new invention. "One size fits all! Superior-quality hosiery that will not run or snag. You can't afford to pass up this offer!!" Give me a break, Barney thought. I wonder if he sat around all day suffering from writer's block as he tried to think that stuff up, or if those catchy phrases came to him naturally.

If you're going to try and sell something as unbelievable as run-proof panty hose, Barney mused, you better get someone like me, a born salesman, someone who could sell ice to the Eskimos, to do it for you. I'll write your ad, I'll even act it. Barney always thought he would have been a great salesman, but his mother said that one

Willy Loman in the family was more than enough and urged him to get into the maintenance workers' union when he had the chance. May she rest in peace, the poor soul.

Barney leaned over and shuffled through the papers. Photocopies of handwritten letters to various hosiery companies asking them for a few minutes of their time were scattered on the table. It doesn't look like he's had to start a file for responses, Barney thought. It'd probably be easier to get an audience with the Pope.

As he straightened up, he scanned the room with his flashlight, and started to walk toward the machines. Before Barney knew what was happening, he tripped over a cardboard box and fell to the floor, his flashlight cracking in the process, tiny pieces of its glass arranging themselves on the floor of the factory. Sharp pain stung his knee and shin. "Damn it! Damn it! Damn! Damn! Damn!" he repeated faster and faster into the sudden darkness as he rolled on his back, cradling his knee to his chest while he rubbed his shin. With his flailing arm he accidentally brushed the side of the cardboard box and grabbed it to steady himself. And then he felt it. And forgot his pain. A jumble of the smoothest, silkiest material skimming his fingertips.

Barney grunted as he lifted his back off the floor and arranged himself Indian-style, with his feet tucked underneath him, then greedily dipped his hands into the mound of luxurious fabric that turned out to be a couple of dozen pairs of panty hose. This must be the stuff, Barney thought. Richie's latest. Knowing that Richie had never been too organized, he helped himself to a few pairs, hoping that they wouldn't be missed. I'll get these home and test these out myself, see if they're what Richie claims they are.

He did.

As far as he could tell, they were.

Run-proof.

Snag-proof.

Which had led him to the Calla-Lily Hosiery Company, whose owner had hired Barney's nephew to do yard work. The only other hosiery company besides the defunct "Hose for the Religious" headquartered in the Miami area. That had been a month ago, and now Barney was waiting to meet with Ruth Craddock for the results of their lab tests.

"Mr. Freize, Ms. Craddock is going to be a little while longer," the receptionist reported to Barney, stirring him out of his thoughts. "Can I get you a cup of coffee?" The request did not sound as if it were coming from an eager-to-please waitress.

How about a life-insurance policy in case I die in this room? Barney thought, but what came out of his mouth was "Light and sweet."

DOWN THE HALL Ruth Craddock sat at the head of the gleaming conference table, panting in exasperation. An ashtray overflowing with cigarette butts smeared with orange lipstick was positioned to her right. She constantly flicked her ever-present cigarette in its general direction, only occasionally hitting the mark. Crushed cans of Coke littered the table. Her ranting speech was interrupted only for deep drags, tornadolike inhales that puckered her weathered cheeks and looked as though they had the force to leave major tar and nicotine deposits in her little toes. Exhales were followed by a swig of soda.

"We are going to get screwed!" she opined in her raspy voice. "We have got to buy the formula for that panty hose or else we'll be out of business! If someone else gets it first, then we may as well put out a sign that says GONE FISHING!''

The eight members of the board seated on either side blanched and shook their heads. They were all older men who had been with Calla-Lily since the early days and were called together now for the first emergency meeting since jeans started to replace skirts in the sixties as the fashion of choice, sending business into a tailspin. Women wanted to be liberated, and one thing they definitely wanted to be liberated from was garters. Garters that dug into the flesh on the backs of their thighs when they were seated, causing pain and leaving indentations. But garters held up stockings, Calla-Lily's bread and butter. That's when the idea of panty hose caught on, thank God, and kept women from adopting jeans or the dreaded pantsuit as permanent replacements for skirts and dresses.

Bra manufacturers had also gone through a worrisome period when their pretty laced cups were being used to fuel bonfires. Fortunately for them, most women realized you can't fight nature and the laws of gravity, and the bra business has held up since then, so to speak.

"I'm telling you," Ruth continued after another drag and swig, "we have got to buy out that Blossom guy before somebody else does. His Birdie Panty Hose is not to be believed. It's comfortable, sexy, can be made in all different colors and, worst of all . . ."

The board members braced themselves.

"IT DOESN'T RUN OR SNAG!"

"But madam," Leonard White, a distinguished octogenarian, began. "Five million dollars is an awful lot of money, and we don't want it to compete with our other lines."

Ruth slammed her fist on the table, causing the ashes to fly around like the fake snow in a watery Christmas-scene paperweight. "What, are you crazy? Who's competing? These panty hose will never see the light of day. Remember our motto: 'Repeat Business.' We buy the formula, own the patent, and then put it away for safe-keeping. Over my dead body will a panty hose be marketed that doesn't run. As for the five million dollars, we figured he could get a lot more than that if it goes to auction. We want to offer him a figure he'll take right away. It'll cost us a lot more than that if someone else gets their hands on it."

White, the only brave one in the group, cleared his throat. "But can we be sure it's so durable? You've only had them for a month."

Ruth narrowed her beady eyes and tossed back her shoulder-length brown hair. "I wore them for a week straight, and went down to wash them in the Laundromat's battered machines every night. Beach towels get chewed up in those things. The next morning when I put them on it was like they were fresh out of the wrapper. Then I gave them to the lab to test. Every test so far has come out positive. Irving is supposed to give us an update at this meeting. WHERE IS HE?"

The door at the back of the room opened and Irving Franklin, a thin, bespectacled man in his early fifties, wearing a white lab coat with a pair of black panty hose draped over his arm, stepped inside. Irving had been with Calla-Lily since the start of his career as an engineer and had seen them through the transition from stockings to panty hose and all the other crises in between, including the year of the fishnets. "Hello, Ruth. I'm here now." There was no trace of nervousness in his manner. He was the one employee Ruth couldn't bully, and she knew it.

"Talk to us, please," Ruth urged. "I've been trying to tell them . . ."

Irving walked to the opposite end of the conference table and reverentially laid the panty hose in front of him. He took off his glasses, pulled a tissue out of his pocket and began to clean them, holding each glass inside his mouth and giving it a good "hahhhhhh," before returning them to the bridge of his nose. The board members fidgeted in their seats and Ruth finally exploded.

"Irving, would you please hurry up!"

Irving stared at her.

Ruth slunk back in her seat.

"I have completed most of the tests," Irving began. "It seems to me we have a breakthrough. I liken this to the discovery of nylon, which of course revolutionized the stocking, for the most part replacing the use of delicate silk. I can't swear, but they seem to be perfect. I even gave them my own personal test."

"What was that?" an up-till-now silent board member croaked in a barely audible voice.

"I lent them to my mother-in-law. She hasn't been to the chiropodist in years."

Murmurs rippled through the boardroom, many of

whose members knew firsthand the importance of monthly visits to the foot clinic.

"My mother-in-law wore these for three days, which is an endurance test equivalent to any of us competing in a triathlon," Irving pontificated as he walked around the room, "and not even breaking a sweat."

More murmurs.

"These panty hose survived so well that my thirteen-year-old daughter, who weighs about one hundred pounds less than her grandmother, was able to borrow them for a teen dance and not worry about bagginess. These things snap right back into shape. Yes, I must say that these are the first 'one size fits all' that don't look cheap."

"I told you!" Ruth yelled. "We've got to buy them before they do to us what nylon did to the silkworm—put it out of a job—"

"However," Irving interrupted, "people's bodies react differently. There's one more endurance test we are now conducting on the pink pair, and our results will not be in until Saturday."

"Saturday!" Ruth screamed. "The panty-hose convention is this weekend. We've got to make a move before Blossom presents them to our competitors. Or, worse yet, peddles them to someone who isn't even in the business, who will put up the money to manufacture them and make a big killing all at once."

"We can't do that until we have the approval of the other board members," Leonard White offered, "and some of them are on vacation. Others are flying in late Friday night."

Ruth crushed another soda can in her hands. "Then we'll have our meeting at the crack of dawn on Saturday . . ."

Several members of the board thought longingly of their golf clubs, which would now go untouched this Saturday morning.

"If we have to, we'll sit here and wait for Irving's results, and then we'll vote. Remember, everyone, we are lucky to be the only company that has the inside scoop on these panty hose. No one else bothered to check them out, probably thought it was some crackpot writing a dopey letter to them." Ruth took a final puff on the little beige stub that was threatening to burn her fingers. "Blossom is planning his fashion show at the convention Saturday afternoon. We've got to get to him before then." She got up and stalked out of the room as the board members gathered around the panty hose in awe.

"I'd a been a lot happier if we had stuck to garters," one was heard to mumble.

WILL EVERYONE PLEASE sit down and be quiet?'' Richie Blossom urged his fellow tenants of the Fourth Quarter old folks' home. ''We have a lot to discuss and not much time left.''

''I've been thinking that for the past twenty years,'' Sam Joggins called out. And then, as everyone expected, went on, ''They call this place the Fourth Quarter. I feel like I'm living in Overtime.'' He slapped his thigh and looked around to see who would laugh this time.

Flo Tides, the social director of the Fourth Quarter, handed Sam a glass of Gatorade in a plastic cup. ''Eb would roll in his grave halfway to China if he heard you. That was his joke.'' Flo continued around the room, handing out the liquid refreshment. Her late husband, Eb, had always been an organizer, and he used to say that the best way to make sure people get to a meeting is to lure them with food and drink. She had met him at a church social fifty years ago, and when they were introduced they both knew they had found the right match. Eb and Flo. And that's what they did together for forty-eight years thereafter.

The twenty-seven people who lived at the Fourth Quarter didn't need to be lured to this meeting by the promise of Gatorade and sprinkled cookies, however, as there was serious business to be discussed. They were in danger of losing their home, the place they had retired to, the place where many of them had found companionship after the death of a spouse. Last year they had purchased an option on the property and that option was about to expire. They had to come up with the money to exercise their option and buy the property outright, but it had to be done by Monday. There was another buyer interested, who already had an offer on the table. And if they gave up their option before the weekend, everyone at the Fourth Quarter would get a bonus check of $10,000.

"Who took the last chocolate cookie?" Elmer Pickett whined as he wandered in and perused the confectionary offerings on the plastic tray. "That always happens to me."

"Well, that's what you get for being late," Flo admonished. "Just take one of the orange ones and sit down. We've got to get started."

"I don't like that kind. The dye runs all over my

tongue," Elmer muttered as he took a seat and crossed his legs.

Richie stood at the front of the room, by the bulletin board that held announcements of upcoming folk dances, poetry readings, and a sign-up sheet for the next outing to Sizzler. He smiled nervously. "Things are tough," he began, "but we've all been through bad times before. We have to stick together. We don't want to lose the Fourth Quarter."

"I say we should take the offer they've made to buy us out," Elmer yelled out. "That way we won't end up with nothing."

"Where we'll end up is living in some dump on the wrong side of the railroad tracks," Richie said vehemently. "I went to check out the place where they want to move us. It's broken down and it stinks."

"Well, at least we'll all go there with a check in our pocket," Elmer cried, still grouchy from not getting a chocolate cookie. "If we don't take their deal right now, then we'll all be tossed out of here with no place to go and no money to get there."

The group started shaking their heads and muttering as Richie called for them to calm down.

"My run-proof panty hose really works. I've got a patent on it. I'm showing it off this weekend at the convention. All the big companies will be there."

"But Richie, your last big invention bombed," Millie Owens choked.

"Do you call the Clapper a bomb? The guy who invented that beat me to the marketplace. My device worked practically the same way."

"Richie, it's easier to clap hands to shut off the television than it is to sneeze it off." Millie snorted.

"Not for people with arthritis," Richie protested.

Flo placed the tray of Gatorade on a side table. "Let's get to the point."

Richie agreed. "Now we all put money into the option. Of course none of us want to lose it. That's why we just have to sit tight until this weekend, when I show the panty hose at the convention."

"But you told us that the panty hose was wonderful and that all the companies would be lining up to buy it," Elmer accused. "What happened to that?"

"I sent them letters, but it's not until they see it that they'll know. That's why we're doing the fashion show. They'll all want it, I'll sell it, and we'll get to stay here. By the end of this weekend I'll be a millionaire and I'll buy this place for all of us. It's our only hope."

Flo interrupted. "Let's get a report from our treasurer."

Nonna Begster stood up with her clipboard in hand and walked to the front of the room. She had an angelic-looking face and graced the group with a beatific smile. Her white cardigan sweater was thrown around her shoulders and buttoned at the neck, leaving its arms dangling at her sides. She cleared her throat and began speaking in a voice that was clear as a bell. "As of three P.M. this afternoon, Eastern Daylight Time, our account at Ocean Savings contained eight hundred twenty-two dollars and seventy-seven cents. This is a result of our bake sale, door-to-door pot-holder drive, and paper-recycling effort. Given that we need one point one million dollars to purchase said property, that leaves us in need of one million, ninety-nine thousand, one hundred seventy-seven dollars and twenty-three cents. Thank you.''

"Give me a break," Elmer yelled. "We've got to win the lottery to raise that much money. Like I said before, we should just take what they're offering and not risk losing everything.''

"I can't stand the idea of leaving this place," Millie Owens moaned sadly. "My son and daughter-in-law would take me in, but they live in Montana and it gets so friggin' cold there.''

"Oh, I know what you mean," Wilhelmina Jackson said enthusiastically. "My daughter-in-law is a pain in my butt.''

Richie interrupted. "If we could all just agree to wait till the end of the weekend and my fashion show, which a few of you ladies have agreed to model in, then I promise you we won't have to leave . . .''

REGAN CHECKED IN at the front desk of the Ocean View Hotel. Walking in the door she felt as if she were stepping into another era. Overhead fans cooled Art Deco furniture. Black-and-white tile covered the floors. Old black-and-white pictures of bathing beauties from the twenties frolicking on the beach across the street hung behind the desk. She handed over her credit card as the dark-skinned girl smiled and looked up Regan's name on the computer. What would we do without computers? Regan thought. Wait on long lines while clerks shuffled through index cards, that's what.

Her room on the second floor was described as having an ocean view—that is if you got out of bed and walked over to the small window in the corner of the room and peered out through the venetian blinds. They should have handed over a periscope with the room key, Regan thought as the bellman placed her luggage on the steel foldout contraption with two army-green threaded belts that somehow held it all together. It screamed for a rest, looking as if it had been salvaged from a Girl Scout camp.

"Thank you," Regan said as she pressed a tip into the bellman's hand.

"You're welcome, miss. Thank you. Enjoy your stay." He shut the door behind him.

Regan looked around the room. It was soothing. A white cotton bedspread, blond pine furniture, an overhead fan above the bed, more pictures of Miami in the old days decorating the walls, all contributed to its charm. A small refrigerator with an ice bucket on top stood in the corner. Regan sat down on the bed and kicked off her shoes. "Thank God," she muttered as she lay back on the bed and stared up at the fan. She closed her eyes for a moment and listened to the faint whir of the blades as they continued on their ever-revolving course. Voices from passersby on the sidewalk one floor down registered in Regan's brain.

Suddenly the phone rang, an urgent double ring, quickly followed by another, as if to admonish the callee to hurry up and answer. Regan sat up.

"Hello."

"Regan, you're there!" It was Maura.

"I just got in a few minutes ago. How are you doing?"

"Well, I'm fine. We're just getting all the last-minute things together. I just talked to your parents over at the

Watergreen. My mother decided to have an impromptu supper here tonight for a few people who are already in town. Luke and Nora said they'd come over, so why don't you come too?''

''Well, sure, I was just going to give them a call to see about dinner.''

''Great. Was your trip all right?''

''Oh, it was fine.''

''How does the bridesmaid dress fit?''

''Like a glove.''

''Oh, that's good, because you know I really tried to pick a dress that you could wear again.''

There was a momentary pause. Regan laughed and so did Maura. ''You don't have to worry about that, Maura. I'm thrilled to be in your wedding, you know that.''

''But really,'' Maura began, ''if you just cut it down, you could wear it to a cocktail party . . .''

Given by who, Regan thought, the Salvation Army? ''Maura!'' she said. ''Stop worrying. It's your day.''

''All right, all right. By the way, do you think you could stop and see if my Uncle Richie is over at the Fourth Quarter? It's just a couple doors down from you. I called his apartment there and got his machine. Sometimes they just sit outside or gather in the community room. We'd love to have him come by tonight. He's been so preoccupied with this panty hose of his that we've hardly seen him, and he probably hasn't been eating right . . .''

''Oh, sure. Then we'll take a cab over to your parents' house.''

"Thanks, Morticia."

"No problem, Wednesday." Regan smiled, remembering their other favorite show, "The Addams Family."

"See you anytime after seven."

"Great." Regan hung up the phone and jumped up. Her jog would have to wait. Time for a quick shower and to pick out the least-wrinkled clothes from her bags. I'm also going to open up one of the bottles of water sitting on the dresser and check if there's any ice in the fridge, she thought. But not before I give Luke and Nora a call.

LUKE AND NORA sat in deck chairs on the balcony of their hotel room, which overlooked the turquoise-blue Atlantic Ocean. They had arrived a few hours before and, following their usual routine, unpacked immediately. Because they did so much traveling, they liked to feel settled in as quickly as possible. Somehow it made hotel rooms feel more homey when you had your own things around.

Nora Regan Reilly, a popular suspense writer, had just completed a book that she claimed had been the most torturous one yet for her to write. Her husband, Luke, and only child, Regan, had reminded her that this was what she said every time she was in the middle of writing a book, and her response was always the same. "It was never this bad." In any case she had happily turned it over to her editor and was very glad to get on the plane with Luke and head to Miami for the funeral convention and Maura's wedding. While Luke attended seminars dealing with the latest embalming techniques, Nora planned to laze by the pool and even squeeze in a massage or two at the hotel health spa. She felt like a hunchback from sitting at her computer for endless hours for the last three months as she revised and re-wrote her latest yarn.

Nora looked over at her husband, who was reading over his notes for the welcome speech he would give tomorrow to his colleagues. Nora smiled as she watched him move his lips, raise his eyebrows, and gesture with his right hand, all without making a sound. "You'd have made a good mime, darling."

"Huh?" Luke looked up from his notes.

"I said, you'd have made a good mime." Nora chuckled and took a sip of her mai-tai.

"Sometimes I feel like a mime. Like when I try to talk our daughter out of taking a dangerous case." Luke shrugged his shoulders, half smiled, and shuffled through his notes. They were both relieved that Regan had just finished a case where she'd been tailing a rapist. The family of one of his victims had been appalled when he was released from prison early on good behavior. They were terrified he would seek revenge on their daughter for testifying in court, so they hired Regan to keep a watch on him. He was moving back to their area. Regan had set herself up as a potential victim in an empty parking lot and nabbed the guy when he tried to force her into her car. He was now back behind bars and wouldn't see the light of day for a long time.

Luke and Nora were proud of her, but still wished she had taken that LSAT course she had signed up for in college and gone on to law school. But one look at the workbook and a few practice tests made Regan realize that she didn't think like a lawyer. She had started training as an investigator when she graduated from college, which over the years had meant a lot of sleepless nights for her parents. They were both looking forward to seeing her and were happy for the chance to have a mini-vacation in Miami this weekend.

The phone rang in their room and Nora put down her drink. "This might be Herself." Nora stepped inside their luxurious hotel room and sat down on the pink pastel couch as she reached for the phone.

Luke cocked his head as he heard his wife of thirty-five years greet their daughter. He turned and saw Nora running her fingers through her short blond hair as she laughed into the phone. Regan, with her dark hair, took after her father, although Luke's had turned to a dignified silver. At six feet five, Luke towered over the five-foot-three Nora. Their offspring combined both sets of genes in the height department, coming in at five feet seven.

Luke stared out in the distance at a ship on the horizon, and then down at the shoreline at a young couple walking the beach with their three small children. He and Nora would have liked to have had a big family but it had never happened for them. That's why it's so nice,

Luke thought, to be down here to celebrate Maura's wedding with the Durkins, people who felt like extended family. Maura and Regan had always been close, and now Maura was marrying a nice guy. Now if only Regan could find someone like that . . . Luke shrugged himself out of his reverie. My God, he thought, I'm starting to think like my beloved wife! Give her a break. If I ever get my hands on that guy who didn't tell her he was engaged, only to let her find out about it by reading it in the Sunday *Times*, I'll kill him. And to think I bought him dinner the week before. He was even marrying someone else named Regan. I guess it makes it easier if you talk in your sleep. But Luke was glad it wasn't his Regan because the guy was such a loser. Regan, of course, had laughed it off, saying she'd been some detective, but in his day . . .

"Hey, Marcel Marceau," Nora said for the second time.

Luke looked up at her. "Very funny."

Nora took his hand and pulled him out of his chair. "We've got to get ready. We're meeting Regan at the Durkins's in less than an hour."

REGAN SHOWERED QUICKLY and immediately felt much better. A cool-water rinse at the end was refreshing and served to give her a second wind. Stepping out of the old-fashioned tub, she wrapped herself in a towel and attempted to wipe the steam off the mirror, only to watch it immediately reappear. I guess I'll get dressed first instead of fighting this losing battle, she thought.

Her garment bag was hanging in the closet, where there was also a safe and, surprisingly enough, a variety of hangers, the kind you'd find in an old closet at home. At least they don't lock them onto the rack the way they do in some hotels, as if anyone paying a couple hundred bucks a night for a room isn't entitled to make off with a few wooden hangers, she thought.

She pulled out a pair of white jeans, a striped blouse
and her red leather flats, then looked at the alarm clock
on the nightstand, which read six-thirty. Regan went
over and picked it up. Boy, this really is a relaxed hotel,
she thought. In most places this thing would be nailed
down with industrial-strength screws. They must have
good insurance.

Ten minutes later, Regan was ready to go. She'd done
a quick makeup job and fluffed her hair with a pick.
She transferred her wallet, keys and a cosmetics bag to
an oversized purse and then decided to take advantage
of the room safe. She placed her extra cash and jewelry
on the shelf, slammed it shut and pulled out the key.
There, she thought, the crown jewels are protected from
any sticky fingers lurking in the vicinity.

She shut the room door and hurried down the one
flight to the main floor. Outside, people were lingering
over drinks at the tables on the sidewalk. One couple
was going through models' composites that were
stacked up before them. Like me going through mug
shots, Regan thought, or police sketches. Only the people I deal with don't have one-word names like Autumn
or Sapphire. South Beach had become the latest hot
spot for fashion shoots. Several young girls with their
portfolios in hand passed her walking down the Strip.

Maura had told her that this place jumps at all hours.
She was right. Now, at six forty-five, it was way too
early for most South Beach diners to have dinner, but
the cafés along Ocean Drive were crowded with people
enjoying a cocktail and checking out the scene. Some
looked very European with their designer shades, and

their cigarettes held at that just-so angle between their fingers.

As Regan strolled along the narrow sidewalk, a dark-haired guy on Rollerblades, wearing a Day-Glo orange outfit, zoomed by her and jumped over one of the small café tables. That lunatic must be getting ready for the Olympics, she thought. He certainly makes walking around here hazardous.

The Fourth Quarter was just two more doors down. There was no missing it. Whereas the other buildings had been transformed into trendy Art Deco pastel treasures, Richie's building looked like a large sea shack. But there was something inviting about it. It looked weather-worn and comfortable. Somehow Regan knew that the people she'd meet inside would not be anything like most of the people she had encountered thus far.

Beach chairs were lined up in a row by the screen door. Regan walked in and was immediately greeted by a diminutive old lady with curly gray hair who was sitting at the front desk with her knitting needles in hand.

"Hello, dear. Can I help you?"

"Yes. I'm looking for Richie Blossom."

"He's at a meeting right now." Knit one, purl two.

"Do you know when he'll be back?" Regan queried.

"He's here, dear." The needles clicked in her skillful hands.

"I'm sorry, I thought you meant he was out."

"Oh, no." The old lady shook her head as if in sympathy.

By the time I figure out Richie's location she'll have

finished an afghan, Regan thought. "Well, then, where is the meeting?"

"Down the hall."

"Do you think I could stick my head in and ask him something?"

"If I sat here all day, I couldn't think of a reason why not." The woman held up the brown square in her hands for inspection.

"Thank you. You say it's right down the hall?"

"Oh, yes. In the room we recently dedicated to Dolly Twiggs, the former owner of the Fourth Quarter, who passed away just a year ago. Keep her in your prayers."

"Of course." Regan smiled and walked toward the back of the building and made a right turn in the paneled hallway, immediately coming upon the Dolly Twiggs Memorial Room. She heard Richie shushing people and begging for order. Regan slipped in the back and took a seat on a folding chair in the corner.

Millie Owens stood up and yelled, "Will everybody please shut up?"

All heads flipped in her direction. "I say let's give Richie a chance. I wouldn't mind a check for ten thousand dollars, but what I want most is to stay here. I've lived here for years and have enjoyed every minute. Like everybody else, I was afraid of getting old, but moving here and being around friends all the time and having socials, I tell you I felt like I was sixteen again. I'd be heartbroken if we had to split up, with some of us ending up in the dump across town and the others being farmed out to relatives. If we take their offer on the option right now, we might get a few dollars, but in the long run we'll have lost something worth a lot more . . .''

The room had grown surprisingly still. You could have heard a pin drop as some of Millie's companions stared at her while others looked down into their laps.

Millie's hands tightened on the chair in front of her. Her face broke into a wry smile. ''Besides, people told me I could have been a model years ago, and now I've got my chance in that fashion show parading around in Richie's panty hose.''

Everyone laughed and the tension in the air seemed to diminish.

Millie continued, ''All of us gals have to get out there on that runway and kick up our heels. The men have to come and support us. And if they end up running us out of here, at least we'll have gone down fighting.'' She sat back down with a defiant look on her face.

Quietly Richie said, ''Thank you, Millie. Now let's take a vote.''

Everyone voted on index cards and they were quickly counted. Twenty-four were in favor of giving Richie a chance to sell the panty hose. Three wanted to surrender the option now. A cheer went up in the room when Richie announced the results.

''Tomorrow afternoon, let's have a rehearsal for the fashion show in here at four P.M. Thanks, everyone.'' Richie hurried to the back of the room and gave Regan a big hug. ''You're here for all the excitement. How are you?''

"I'm fine, Richie. Maura called and they're having dinner at the house, but she couldn't reach you. Can you come with me now?"

"You bet, honey, you bet."

Regan and Richie walked arm in arm back up the paneled hallway. "Regan, do you mind coming up to my apartment for a minute? I want to grab a light jacket."

"Sure."

They walked up the curving staircase to Richie's second-floor apartment.

"Regan, I tell you, this is going to be some weekend for excitement," Richie said as he put the key in the door.

"Maura told me about your panty hose," Regan said as she followed him inside.

"I tell you, honey, they're unbelievable. Wait here a second," he said and disappeared into the bedroom.

Regan heard him rummaging around and sat down on the overstuffed couch, next to a black-and-white wedding picture of Birdie and Richie.

A minute later Richie was back, handing Regan several pairs of the magic panty hose. "Here, try them. This is one invention of mine that really works."

Regan held the luxuriant fabric in her fingers. "They're beautiful, Richie."

"They're not just beautiful. They last and last. There's a panty-hose convention over at the Watergreen Hotel this weekend, and I'm arranging a fashion show so the big shots can get an idea of what I'm offering here. All I need is the chance to show it off and I'll get the money to save this place. They'll all be fighting to buy the patent I have on them.''

"They're so delicate," Regan murmured as she admired both the ivory and pale-pink colors.

"They come in all different colors. Do you think your mother would like a pair?"

"Sure. She's always complaining that she can't find a pair of panty hose that fit decently and won't run."

"Let me grab a few more."

Regan pulled on the fabric and was amazed that something that looked so fragile seemed so resilient.

Richie reappeared with his hands full. "I'll just carry these."

"Here," Regan said. "Put them in my bag. It's oversized anyway."

"Oh, one more thing," Richie said. He looked over at the corner table and saw that the light on the answering machine was blinking. "I'd better check my messages." He hurried over and pushed the playback button.

There were two messages from Maura, one hang-up, and one from the Models Models Modeling Agency. A gruff woman's voice barked, "Richie, this is Elaine. If you weren't so adorable, I'd think I was crazy. I've got some of the models coming by your place tomorrow for you to see about the fashion show. I told them they won't get paid unless you sell the panty hose, but they're willing to take the chance. They're young, they like you, and what the hell, the show's on a Saturday anyway.

It's six o'clock and I'm going home. Give me a call tomorrow.''

Richie rewound the tape and chuckled. "Regan, I bet you didn't know I'm about to become a star. A photographer needed some extras for a shoot they were doing on the beach and they wanted some of us old guys for authenticity and I got picked.'' He laughed as he gathered up his jacket. "He said I was a natural, so I went down to this modeling agency to see if they'd be interested in representing me—and they were. Said they needed a few different types besides the gorgeous young girls. Elaine sent me out on a commercial audition for a local restaurant and I got the job! Now they're willing to help me out with my fashion show.''

"I'd better get your autograph now!" Regan laughed.

Richie shut the door and they started walking downstairs. "The commercial is supposed to start airing any day now. It's so much fun. I've become friendly with the people at the agency and it gives me something else to do, besides my inventions. Since Birdie died, I just like to keep busy . . .''

"I know," Regan said softly as they reached the sidewalk and felt the salty breeze blow up from the ocean. They walked quietly for a moment, then stepped off the curb to cross the street. Richie turned to her as they continued walking. From behind him Regan could see a dark car speeding up the side street. "RICHIE, WATCH OUT!" she screamed as she pulled him back to the sidewalk and they both tumbled to the ground. The car's front wheel screeched against the curb as it hurtled past them and disappeared around the corner and down Ocean Drive. For a moment they both lay dazed on the sidewalk. That guy deliberately tried to hit us, Regan thought, as she pulled herself to a sitting position. People were rushing over to assist them to their feet.

"Richie, are you all right?" Regan asked.

"Yeah, sure, thanks to you, Regan," he said fervently.

A pretty young girl who looked like a model was picking something up in the street. "Is this your bag?" she asked.

"What's left of it," Regan said as she studied the squashed white tote with the tire mark down the center. She bent down and gathered up the panty hose that had fallen out and had been run over.

"You two sure were lucky," a middle-aged man in the crowd called out.

"Did anybody get a good look at the car or the driver?" Regan asked.

People in the crowd shook their heads. "It all happened so fast," a waiter from the café nearby said. "It's too bad there wasn't more traffic. He'd have been slowed up, but he got away before anyone realized what happened."

"It was a he?" Regan asked quickly.

"Yes, a dark-haired guy in a blue sedan."

The crowd started to break up as the shock of what almost happened began to wear off.

"If anyone remembers anything about the car or the driver that might be helpful, please let me know," Regan called out. "My name is Regan Reilly and I'm staying at the Ocean View. That did not seem like an accident."

She turned to Richie and held out the stained ivory panty hose. "I'm so sorry."

"No problem, Regan," Richie replied and started to brush off the fabric. Amazingly the dirt disappeared. "See!" he said. "It's like the commercial with the gorilla who jumps all over the suitcase. You can't hurt it!"

"Too bad you can't say the same for us," Regan said as she rubbed her knee. The encounter with the sidewalk had torn her white jeans, leaving them slightly bloodied. "Let's get out of here. They're going to be wondering what happened to us."

"We can tell them we were testing my panty hose," Richie said brightly.

"That sounds like a good explanation for my parents," Regan said as she steered him across the street to the taxi stand, checking both directions before they moved an inch.

THE CAR THAT had almost hit Richie and Regan made a quick right turn off Ocean Drive. The driver raced the two blocks to Washington Avenue as he pounded his fist against the steering wheel. Heading north, a few blocks later he spotted a parking space and quickly pulled over. Within seconds Judd Green had peeled off his windbreaker, stuffing it into a gym bag on the floor of the stolen car.

He looked around quickly, made certain he was not being observed, then leaned down and yanked off the dark wig that was covering his blond hair, placing it in the bag with the windbreaker. Sliding over to the passenger side, he got out, picked up his bag, pulled off his gloves, and joined the thin stream of pedestrians, just another lean, tanned, good-looking male in his early thirties. A closer examination would have revealed the cold emptiness of his brown eyes, the raw strength of his shoulder and arm muscles.

He walked as quickly as he dared without attracting notice for a mile, until he reached the Watergreen Hotel. Sidling in the front door, Green took the stairs to his tenth-floor room, where he hid the gym bag in the closet, ran his head under the faucet and quickly changed into khakis and a sport shirt. He combed back his wet hair, sprayed on cologne, gathered up his wallet, and headed out to the elevator bank.

Two middle-aged couples were greeting each other, saying how quickly the year had gone since the last convention. They all wore badges indicating they were in town for the gathering of morticians. He smiled at them and pretended to be absorbed in his own thoughts as he listened to them yak about their plans for the weekend. I wish I could have served you up some business, fellas, he thought grimly, but I blew it. For now.

Downstairs in the lobby he ordered a beer at the bar and made it a point to flirt with the tawny blonde a few stools away who had placed her towel near his on the beach that morning. He chatted with the bartender, who told him he'd been at the Watergreen for thirty years and proceeded to ramble on about how many hurricanes he had sat out in this very lobby.

"In my time here," the short dark-haired man with a slight Spanish accent said cheerfully as he wiped off the bar, "I have seen some unbelievable things go on. My wife says I should write a book, but I don't want to lose my job."

"I bet," he said.

"Yeah, like this weekend, we've got two conventions. Funeral people and panty-hose people. Now if they're going to have a few fitting sessions with the girls in their panty hose, I say great. Which room? Can I deliver the drinks? But I can do without seeing people check out how good coffins fit. I guess we all have to go sometime . . ."

"Right, buddy." He laid his money on the bar and got up to leave. I've been here long enough to establish my presence, he thought. He headed around the corner, into the area where the pay phones were lined up. Sliding into a booth, he shut the door and braced himself for the call he had to make.

The phone rang three times before it was picked up.

"It didn't work," Green said flatly. "He was walking with some girl. She pushed him out of the way." He gripped the receiver and listened.

"No, I don't know who she was. But don't worry. It's not going to happen again. Next time I'll get both of them."

THE TAXI PULLED up in front of the Durkin home. A beautiful stucco ranch house, it reminded Regan of the kind of homes you find in southern California.

Richie insisted on paying for the cab, saying never in his life would he let a lady pay his way.

"Forget your inventions; you should start a charm school for men," Regan said as she got out of the car. "And I'll give you a few names for your mailing list."

They rang the bell and stood waiting as they heard voices on the inside. Mr. Durkin, an auburn-haired man of medium height with the map of Ireland on his face, answered the door and extended his arms. "Regan, Richie, come in. We've been waiting for you," he boomed in a voice never used at the Durkin Funeral Home.

He hugged both of them. They were barely in the door when Richie began telling him about their adventure. "You'll never believe what happened. We were almost killed. If it weren't for Regan's quick thinking . . ."

Nora and Luke, followed by members of the Durkin clan, hurried from the living room into the foyer when they heard the commotion.

"Hey, everybody," Regan said brightly and went over to kiss her parents.

"Regan, what happened to your pants?" Nora asked.

Regan looked down at her knee, which was bloodier-looking than before.

"She almost got killed trying to save my life," Richie said with enthusiasm. "You should be so proud of her."

"Oh, God, Luke, I thought this was going to be a vacation," Nora moaned. "Regan, are you okay?"

"Oh, Mom, it was no big deal. We were waiting to cross the street and a car came by going a little fast, that's all. I pulled Richie out of the way and we both fell down."

"What's going on?" Maura called out as she entered the room from the kitchen. "Oh, good, Regan and Richie are finally here."

"Regan just saved me from being killed," Richie insisted on repeating, much to Regan's chagrin.

"What?" Maura exclaimed.

"We were outside and a car came speeding by and Regan pushed me out of the way." Richie sounded as though he was just getting warmed up.

Ed Durkin suddenly urged everyone to move into the

living room. "Have a drink, for God's sake, tonight is a celebration."

As everyone wandered back into the large living room, Regan and Maura hugged.

"Let me get you a drink," Maura urged. "Still drinking white wine?"

"Of course," Regan replied and sat down on the couch next to her parents.

"You know, dear, you could stay in our room tonight. Maybe that would be a good idea," Nora suggested.

"Mom, chances are I'm not going to get killed escorting Richie back."

Richie plopped down in the chair across from them as Maura returned with Regan's drink. He began his fourth recitation of the near tragedy.

"My God, Richie, isn't it just about a year ago that Dolly Twiggs was murdered?" Maura asked.

"Murdered?" Regan echoed.

"We don't think she was murdered," Richie said, "but yes, it was just about a year ago she died. We're having a memorial service in the Dolly Twiggs Memorial Room on Monday."

"The cops think she was murdered," Maura reminded him.

"What happened to her?" Regan asked quickly.

"She liked to take early-morning walks on the beach. A group of sunrise swimmers found her face-down in shallow water. There was a bump on her head and some blood, but it could have been from hitting a rock when she went down. Dolly actually died of drowning, so she had to have been breathing when she hit the sand," Richie reported. "She had a heart attack. Her jewelry was missing."

"That's too bad," Regan murmured, as all her instincts warned her that it sounded like more than a mugging.

"We were just lucky," Richie continued, "that she had signed the deal giving us the year-long option the day before she died. She wasn't supposed to sign it until the next day, but the nice young man from the real estate office brought it over for her on his way home from work. It gave us a year to raise the money to buy the place. Otherwise we probably would have had to get out right away. So now, if my panty hose takes off on Saturday—"

"Who was the guy from the real estate office?" Regan asked.

"I was sitting at the front desk that day when he came by. We all take turns. I think he said his name was Joey."

Regan immediately thought of her gum-chomping seatmate, Nadine, whose boyfriend Joey worked in a real estate office. She made a mental note to check it out first thing in the morning.

"Richie," Regan said. "Get out your panty hose." She turned to her mother. "Mom, what do you think of hosting a cocktail party on Saturday afternoon, before a panty-hose fashion show?"

NICK FARGUS SAT at his desk in the manager's office of the Watergreen Hotel. He liked to think of himself as the captain of a ship. The one-thousand-room hotel with its many conference rooms, ballrooms, restaurants and arcade of shops all hummed around him. It was always busy but especially in the winter months, when they were booked solid with conventions. One after another. Wanting to escape the dismal cold and slushy streets up yonder, conventioneers came down to Miami anxious to soak up the sun and play a few rounds of golf or tennis, often abandoning the idea of attending unnecessary seminars or meetings.

And it wasn't only the weather. Miami had become a real international hot spot, a center for culture. In the past few years it had experienced dynamic growth, and the future looked even better. Designers, musicians, dancers, photographers and models were all setting up shop down here. Celebrities were jetting in for the weekends. Even Madonna had bought an estate. Things were happening. There was a beat that was getting louder, and people from all over the world were hearing it.

So why did Nick feel so out of it?

Because of South Beach, or SoBe, as it was also known these days.

Just a few miles down the road, it felt like a different world from the Watergreen. It was where all the hip and beautiful people stayed, where they strolled, where they partied. Hell, the Watergreen made the best piña colada in Florida, but it wasn't as much of a draw anymore. Everyone was drinking all that annoying mineral water. The Watergreen had a great piano bar but the models weren't interested in sitting around and listening to show tunes. They just wanted to go to those clubs where they pack you in and blare the music.

At forty-two, with sandy hair, mild gray eyes and a slight build, nothing about Nick attracted immediate attention. He made a good living and had socked away some money but he never felt content. Sure, on some days he felt like Donald Trump as he blustered around the hotel solving problems, his phone ringing endlessly. But on nights like last night, when he had gone down to South Beach for a drink and the models he met wouldn't give him more than three seconds of their time, he felt angry. If I were a club owner, they wouldn't treat me that way, he thought. He was feeling so bad he went into one of the shops and bought a hot new skin cream that cost a fortune.

Nick straightened the papers on his desk and took a final sip from his coffee. It was nearly eight o'clock. What should he do tonight?

Never having married, Nick was always looking for a woman who could advance his social position. Along the way there'd been a few nice girls he had dated, but they all wanted to settle down and have children, and that didn't cut the mustard with him. "I'm not ready," he told those types. One had recently replied, "You're going to have to chase your kids around the house with a walker."

Nick got up from his desk and turned out the lights of his office. One of the perks of his job was to have his own large apartment on the top floor of the hotel. Very impressive. If I could only get one of those models to see it, he thought, then they'd look at me with different eyes. So far, no such luck.

I'm not that hungry, he thought. And I don't feel like watching television. Maybe I'll put on that new flowery shirt I bought for $175 at one of those fancy boutiques and give South Beach another try tonight. Who knows? Maybe I'll finally get lucky.

REGAN SAT IN the lobby of the Ocean View enjoying her morning coffee and a bowl of fruit. Breakfast was an informal buffet where you helped yourself to coffee and juice and chose from a variety of cereals, bread and fruit. Bacon and eggs had to be specially ordered from the kitchen, but you'd be hard-pressed to find anyone in this crowd to admit they ate such cholesterol-laden no-no's.

Glancing through the Miami paper, Regan read about the usual assortment of crimes that you'd find in almost any big city's newspaper. Robberies, murders, drug deals gone bad, arson. A new favorite in Miami was to bump the car in front of you at a stoplight. When the driver gets out to check for damage, someone else comes out of nowhere, reaches in the window and grabs purses, briefcases, whatever he can get his hands on. In really bad neighborhoods you were encouraged to hand over your wallet by the barrel of a gun. Regan folded the paper. Thank God there wasn't an article about a successful hit-and-run on Ocean Drive last night.

On the way home Richie had told her the name of the real estate agency that was handling the option on the Fourth Quarter. It was called the Golden Sun. Regan had looked up its address and was happy to discover that it was only a few blocks away. She planned on making a little visit there this morning.

I should have taken Nadine's number, Regan thought. But hopefully she'd find Nadine's Joey at the Golden Sun and get some information out of him. Dolly Twiggs's suspicious death and the near accident last night, both around the times of real estate transactions, were a little coincidental for her taste. Transactions having to do with valuable waterfront property in a booming area.

The big clock on the wall read ten-fifteen.

At ten-thirty Regan walked up the steps to the Golden Sun. It was actually a small white house off Washington Avenue. Inside Regan found a pleasant-looking guy with a baby face sitting behind the receptionist's desk.

"Hot enough for you?" he joked.

"Yes, actually it is getting a little warm out there, isn't it?" Regan agreed.

"Unusual for November. But I say it beats the cold. That's why we're always so busy. People realizing that they want to throw away their snow shovels and enjoy nice weather year round. Is that why you're here?''

"Actually, I was looking for someone named Joey.''

"That's me.''

"Oh, are you Nadine's boyfriend?'' Regan asked.

"The only one, I hope. How did you know? No, don't tell me. You're the one who sat next to her on the plane yesterday.''

"That's right,'' Regan laughed. "By the way, thanks for the ride into town.''

"No problem. Nadine's got me trained. She told me all about you, that you're here for a wedding and that you're a detective.'' His eyes sparkled.

The phone rang and Joey held up his finger. "Just a sec, Regan.''

Boy, Regan thought, he even knows my name. She turned to glance out the window and saw Nadine teetering up the block in stiletto heels and chewing on a piece of gum. As Joey finished up his conversation, Regan watched Nadine spit her gum into a tissue and shove it into the side pocket of her purse.

"Here comes Nadine,'' Regan announced.

"Oh, good, she was coming down to join me for my coffee break. She'll be real glad to see you.''

"Hi, Regan,'' Nadine said breathlessly as she came through the door. "I was going to stop by your hotel after coffee.'' She went over and gave Joey a kiss.

"Nadine, I smell spearmint.''

"Breath candy, Joey, breath candy.'' Nadine turned and winked at Regan. "I always carry it around but am afraid to offer it to people because they always think it's because they need it I'm offering. Sometimes that's the case, but mostly it's just to be polite.'' She pulled them out of her purse. ''Want one, Regan?''

Regan blinked. ''Sure.''

''Are you coming with us for coffee?'' Nadine asked.

''I was just about to ask her, dollface,'' Joey said quickly. ''How about it, Regan? We never got around to talking about why you stopped by in the first place. Or how you even found out where I work.''

''She's a detective, Sherlock.'' Nadine pinched his cheek.

Regan laughed. ''I'd love to join you, as long as I'm not intruding.''

''No way,'' Nadine insisted.

Good, Regan thought. I really want to talk to this guy, and what better way than over coffee?

In the coffee shop down the street Regan sat across the booth from Nadine and Joey. They were served immediately, and as Regan stirred her third cup of the day, she commented that she and Joey know someone in common.

''Who?'' Joey asked.

''Richie Blossom. He lives at the Fourth Quarter.''

''Oh, yeah. He's a nice fellow.''

Regan took a sip and placed her cup back on its saucer. ''He said that you saved the people who live there from losing the place last year.''

Joey shrugged his shoulders. ''The owner lived there but couldn't keep up with paying all the repairs. But she didn't want her friends to be kicked out. So she decided to option the place to them and give them a year to come up with the money. We drew up the agreement and she was supposed to come over here the next day to sign it. I decided to just take it with me when I left work and stop there on the way home. I guess you heard she died the next morning.''

"Yes, I did," Regan said.

Nadine had become very quiet, her eyes darting back and forth as they talked.

"Dolly Twiggs was a decent woman," Joey said matter-of-factly. "She could have gotten a lot more money for that place than she was going to sell it to them for. But she said one point one million dollars was all she would ever need and these people were like family to her. If those papers hadn't been signed, then chances are that place would have been scooped up immediately. I'm sure you know what's happening with real estate around here, especially beachfront property.''

"I've heard," Regan said. "Did you spend much time with her when you went over there that day?"

Joey leaned back in the booth and played with his spoon. "I went up to her apartment. Her sister was there. They both collected seashells. They were all over the place. I sat on one and it broke. They said not to worry because they always took a six A.M. walk together every morning and that was the best time to find more.''

"Her sister?" Regan asked. "I didn't know she had a sister.''

"She was in town for a visit. They both were going

to take off on a three-month cruise. A lot of cruise ships leave out of the Port of Miami."

"I thought Dolly was by herself when she died."

"She was. Her sister wasn't feeling well that morning and decided to sleep in. Needless to say, she was devastated."

Regan shifted in her seat. "Where is her sister now?"

"She ended up going on that cruise by herself and then went home to Dallas. Said she felt too sad being around here, although I understand she's coming into town this weekend for a memorial service."

"So when the place is sold, the money will go to her?" Regan asked.

"She's not looking to get rid of the people there, but she can't afford to keep up the place either. The taxes around here have gone crazy. From what everybody says, the residents of the Fourth Quarter can't come up with the money, so it's going to end up going to somebody else."

"Your office is handling it?"

"We handled the option and we also have people who are willing to put up a lot of money for it as soon as it's free. We even have somebody who's willing to pay them a bonus if they give it up before the weekend. But if Twiggs's sister has somebody else who wants to buy it, she doesn't necessarily have to go through us. So we could make a killing, or we could lose everything. But let me tell you something," Joey said as he looked directly into Regan's eyes. "I was happy I brought over that option when I did. My boss wasn't too thrilled because we probably could have made a sale right away so they could settle the estate. I want to make a lot of money just as much as everybody else does. But all I could think about was what if it was my own grandmother in the same situation? I wouldn't want her to lose her home.''

Nadine kissed him on the cheek. "See why I love this guy?"

"I sure do," Regan said as Joey checked his watch.

"I've got to get back to work."

"I'm going to the beach," Nadine pronounced. "Want to come, Regan?"

"I've got a few things to do, Nadine, but give me your number and maybe we can get together later." Regan was very anxious to head back to the Fourth Quarter and find out about Dolly Twiggs's sister.

IRVING FRANKLIN LOVED his mini laboratory in the basement of his home. Not only did it allow him to continue his experiments away from work but it also provided an escape for him from the annoyances of family life. Not that he didn't love his family, but with his mother-in-law living under the same roof, his nerves were much more easily frayed.

It was Friday morning and he had just come down the steps to check on the panty hose that he had left steeping overnight in a Crockpot full of harsh chemicals. He pulled off the lid and with a large set of tongs extricated a lump of hose from the bubbling container. In awe he watched them dry off almost immediately and look as good as new.

"Damn," he muttered. "These can't be for real. There's got to be something wrong with them."

With that the basement door was flung open and his mother-in-law yelled down, "Let's go, Irving. Did you forget you're supposed to drop me off at the doctor on your way to work?"

Irving shuddered. He felt as if his day had been ruined.

"IRVING! Did you hear me?"

"Get in the car!" he yelled back as he dropped the hose in a plastic bag and set off for what was usually a pleasant commute to work.

INSIDE DOLLY TWIGGS'S apartment, her sister Lucille Coyle turned on the gas jet underneath the kettle. She jumped back as the flame leapt upward, igniting with a miniature boom. Oh, my, I forgot about that, she thought. She adjusted the pilot and looked around. Everything felt a little dusty. Neglected-looking. Well, it has been just a year since Dolly breathed her last, Lucille thought.

A wave of sadness passed through Lucille, almost freezing her in place. Tears stung her eyes. I've got to get busy, she thought. It's the only thing that makes you feel better at a time like this.

She ran water over a shriveled orange sponge and smiled as it puffed up before her. Humming to herself one of her favorite hymns from church, she wiped the

counters in the cozy kitchen. Poor Dolly, she thought
as she straightened the decorative jars labeled FLOUR,
SUGAR, COFFEE, TEA. I always tried to get her to put
these on the other counter and have the toaster over
here. It would have made so much more sense. And the
glasses should have been right over the sink, where you
can reach them if . . .

The doorbell rang. Lucille muttered, "Wonder who
that could be," put down the newly vitalized sponge,
and futzed with her hair as she walked across the living
room to the front door. She pulled it open and gushed
when she saw who was standing in front of her.

"Richie, how are you? You look wonderful. Please
come in. And who do you have here?"

"Hello, Lucille," Richie said quickly, kissing her on
the forehead. "I'm so glad you made it here for the
memorial service. This is my friend Regan Reilly. She's
in Miami for my niece's wedding."

"How nice. Would you two like a cup of tea? I'm
just making a pot. I also picked up some lovely jelly
doughnuts on the way in from the airport."

"That sounds great," Regan said, smiling at the
thought of all the people who thought you had to eat
alfalfa sprouts and yogurt to live a long life. Lucille
had to be in her eighties and she obviously relished
junk food. It just goes to show that being uptight about
eating all the right foods is worse for your health than
munching a jelly doughnut and enjoying every minute
of it.

Lucille fluttered into the kitchen as Richie and Regan

made themselves comfortable. Regan looked around at the seashell decor and smiled. "When I was little and we went to the beach, I'd collect a whole bunch of shells and bring them home. Maura and I used to sit in the backyard and hold them up to our ears to see if we could hear the sounds of the ocean."

"The surf crashing . . ." Richie agreed.

"Well, actually I think we picked up a little interference from the Jersey Turnpike. But then we'd paint them with watercolors and douse them with some god-awful glitter and give them away as presents. Talk about destroying the natural beauty of this planet. We were an ecologist's worst nightmare."

"They were cute," Richie insisted. "You sent one to me and Birdie for our anniversary. I still have it."

Lucille reappeared, carefully carrying a tray of jig-gling teacups, a matching flowered teapot, a creamer and sugar bowl, and a plate of doughnuts. She ceremoniously placed it on the coffee table with the lace doilies. "Here we go." She poured two cups and handed them to Regan and Richie.

Richie helped himself to a doughnut. "Do you know what kind of jelly is in here?"

"Raspberry."

"That's my favorite."

"Mine, too," Regan said as she settled back with her first jelly doughnut in about eight years.

"Regan is a detective," Richie began.

"Oh, my," Lucille said as she sipped her tea.

Regan took a deep breath. "I'm not in Miami on

business, but last night Richie and I were almost run down by a car outside here—''

''You were what?'' Lucille interrupted, her expression aghast.

''We were on our way to Richie's niece's house when I think a car intentionally tried to hit us. I understand your sister was mugged on the beach right across the street from here. I couldn't help but wonder if there was any connection. Richie thought it would be all right to talk with you.''

Lucille's eyes clouded. It was still so hard for her to talk about Dolly without getting a lump in her throat. But she didn't want anyone else to get hurt, so she'd do her best.

''I understand it was quite a shock when she died,'' Regan gently prodded.

''Oh, Lord, yes. Whenever I visited, I used to love to walk the beach with her in the early morning. We were all set to go on a cruise together. I had flown in the day before to stay for a few days before our trip. She had made chow mein for dinner. Well, it's not really chow mein, but she loved to call it that. What you do is take a cup of Minute Rice, two tablespoons of soy sauce—''

''I remember Dolly used to make that,'' Richie interrupted.

''Right,'' Lucille continued. ''Now normally Dolly was a good cook, but the next morning I wasn't feeling quite up to par. I had just flown in from Dallas and flying is a little dehydrating and I had had a few glasses of wine, so maybe that's why I didn't feel like getting up for our walk, but I wasn't up to it, you know what I mean.''

"Of course," Regan answered.

"Anyway, she was gone for what seemed like a long time to me, and I got up and went downstairs and there was a commotion across the street, and oh, my God . . ." Tears filled Lucille's eyes. "Dolly was dead on the beach. Her little diamond earrings were ripped out of her ears and her wedding ring, which she never took off, was gone, and so was her birthstone ring. The seashells from her tote bag were scattered around her and her change purse was missing. She always brought it with her so she could pick up some nice hot rolls from the bakery on the way back." Lucille paused. Her voice quivered as she said, "Dolly was face-down in the sand. Her forehead had blood all over it.''

"I understand she had a heart attack," Regan said quietly.

"Who wouldn't have a heart attack when somebody tries to attack you?" Lucille asked, exasperated.

"She had never had dizzy spells or a problem with her heart before?"

"Not at all," Lucille said firmly. "She was like an ox. Right, Richie?"

Richie swallowed the last bite of his jelly doughnut. "Right. She used to haul out all the folding chairs for our meetings herself. She was always doing, doing, doing.''

"So she'd never been sick?" Regan asked.

Lucille shook her head. "No . . . well, except for the time she got a piece of glass in her hand when she was washing the dishes at my place. We were using Mama's delicate china and glassware and Dolly insisted on doing it all herself because one time one of our guests tried to help and dropped a glass and we were heartbroken because it broke up the set of eight. Well, Dolly was there washing the dishes and one of the glasses broke and she got a little sliver of glass in her hand that didn't all come out, but she didn't feel it for so long, and then, when she came back to Miami, she had to have an operation to get it out and I had to fly back from Dallas to take care of her, and oy vay.''

"Hmmmm," Regan said, then tried to steer the subject back to the incident on the beach. "Was there any sign of anything that could have been used to hit her on the head?" Regan asked.

"She had landed headfirst on a rock. They don't know whether that's what made her bleed or if the mugger had hit her with it and dropped it. But the funny thing was it was a big rock and not the kind you usually see on the beach. But to murder her for a little bit of jewelry and small change? Why?" Dolly asked and looked upward, shaking her head. "Maybe it was somebody who was crazed and on drugs.''

Or maybe, Regan thought, it was somebody who wanted to make it look like a robbery when the motivation was something else. "Was there ever any talk of the possibility that she had a heart attack and fell over and someone came by and stole her jewelry? That type of thing happens a lot with car-accident victims.''

"Not really. I would like to think that that's what

happened, that she died of natural causes. But in my heart I don't think that's what happened."

I don't either, Regan thought. "It must be hard for you," she said.

"She was all I had left. I haven't been here since she died because it's just too painful. Everything here is a reminder of her. That's why I'm hoping that Richie here can pull off his sale of the panty hose this weekend. I would love for the residents to buy this place, but if they can't, I have to sell it to someone else. I can't afford to keep it up and I just want to be finished with it. I want to get back to Dallas, where my friends are." Lucille blushed. "I also have a lovely gentleman friend back there waiting for me. Arthur Zipp. We met on a bus trip to the Alamo six months ago and have been keeping company ever since."

"Oh, that's nice," Regan said gently.

Lucille smiled. "And if I don't hurry back, I know that some of the other gals from our church group are going to start making casseroles for him. Moving in on Arthur, you know what I mean, Regan?"

"I know what you mean," Regan laughed, thinking of all the times she'd been to cocktail parties, ended up next to some guy, so you introduced yourselves to each other, and before you could say "Beam me up, Scottie," his wife or girlfriend materialized at his side, like a homesteader with a shotgun. Protecting her territory even though no attack had been planned. I can only imagine what would have happened if I were holding a casserole, Regan thought.

"When Birdie died I got a lot of casseroles and home-made cakes," Richie offered. "The only trouble was I didn't feel like eating. Regan, I've got to get over to the agency. Are you still interested in coming?"

"Yes, Richie; but Lucille, one more thing. Were there any newspaper accounts of her death?"

"A few in the drawer, including an obituary."

"May I borrow them? I'd just like to look them over."

"Of course. I'd be only too happy to find out who did that to Dolly." Lucille went over to the antique desk, pulled an envelope with the clippings out of a drawer, and handed it over to Regan. "Like the Lord says, the truth shall set us free."

"I'll get these back to you right away."

"Don't worry. I'll be here all weekend. God willing."

THE CALLA-LILY Hosiery Company had taken a suite at the Watergreen Hotel, setting up its world headquarters there for the duration of the panty-hose convention. Since their home base was Miami, the powers that be at Calla-Lily, namely Ruth Craddock, felt it was not necessary to pay for rooms for their employees to stay overnight. This even though these same employees were expected at all functions ranging from early-morning breakfast meetings to late-night powwows on how to improve sales in tropical countries.

But things were not going smoothly this Friday morning. Ruth, known as Ruthless by her long-suffering underlings, was on a rampage trying to locate the missing board members whose presence was necessary for the vote on Saturday. Somewhere amid the swirls of gray smoke, she was screaming into a telephone.

"What do you mean, he's bushwhacking his way through mountainous terrain on a mule in the wilderness! Track him and his backpack down and get him onto a plane! Let him bring the mule with him if he wants!" Ruth steadied herself and took a deep drag from her cigarette. "I don't care if he's pursuing a lifelong dream! If he wanted to find himself, he should have started looking before his eighty-third birthday!" She slammed down the phone.

"Ruth," her assistant, Ethel, said nervously, "you are due to give a speech in ten minutes."

"Which speech was that?" Ruth asked impatiently.

" 'Knee-highs as a fashion statement. Fact or fantasy?' "

"Where are my notes?"

"Right here."

"Have we heard from Irving?"

"Not a word."

"Ethel, you knew Grandpa," Ruth said.

"Of course; I was his secretary for many years."

"Don't you think I know that?" Ruth screamed. "You know, Ethel, the trouble is people just don't care anymore. They don't care that Grandpa built this business up from stitching together socks at the dining-room table. They don't care. They just collect their paychecks every week and let Calla-Lily be damned. But if we go out of business, with this run-proof panty hose coming out, they'll be sorry."

Ethel shook her head mournfully, tsk-tsking as Ruth

extinguished her cigarette and applied a fresh coat of lipstick.

"Your grandpa was very proud of you, Ruth, the way you took over the business. He was a very good man. He could get a little pushy at times—"

"Ethel," Ruth interrupted as she snapped her purse shut, "I'll be back in an hour, and hopefully there will be some happy messages for me."

If not, Ethel thought, I'll make some up myself.

NICK FARGUS WAS not in a very good mood. Last night he had barely sat down at one of the cafés on Ocean Drive when a waiter came by and lost his balance, spilling a bowl of capellini pomodoro onto his new shirt. In English, Nick thought, that means red spaghetti sauce that produces a very stubborn stain. The worst part of it was that Nick was sure that a girl sitting a few tables away had been eyeing him. She looked like she could be one of the models. By the time he had hurried home, changed and raced back, she was gone. Only later did it occur to him that he should have just gone next door and treated himself to another shirt. Those boutiques were open all night.

Sighing, Nick sat down at his desk. It was going to

be a very busy weekend with the two conventions. They had already had problems with overbooking. Too many fires to put out, and he had to be on twenty-four-hour duty. Now he wouldn't get back down to South Beach until next week.

Already that morning he had been awakened from a sound sleep by a panicked phone call from the front desk. Coffins were being wheeled through the lobby to the display room for the funeral convention, upsetting some of the guests. Told to use the service entrance, the offenders argued that they had seen mannequins wearing nothing but panty hose being traipsed through the day before, and no one had seemed to mind.

Nick's intercom buzzed.

What now? he thought as he picked up his phone.

"Mr. Fargus?"

"Yes, Maria." Nick rubbed his head.

"One of our guests would like to see you." Maria sounded excited.

Another problem, he thought. It's too early for this. "Tell them I'm tied up right now, but I'll see them later."

"Mr. Fargus, she's right here. It's rather important."

"Okay, send her in." Nick knew that he could trust Maria's judgment. He was lucky to have a secretary like her. She only bothered him with big things, taking care of minor problems herself.

An instant later the door opened and Maria walked in and beamingly introduced Nora Regan Reilly. ". . . And, Mrs. Reilly, this is Nick Fargus."

Nick shook Nora's hand. "Nice to meet you, Nora Regan Reilly. Say, your name sounds familiar."

Maria shot a reproachful glance at him. "Mrs. Reilly writes suspense novels." She turned to Nora. "I love your books. I have all of them."

"Thank you."

Nick jumped in. "Oh, of course. That's why your name sounded familiar. You see, I don't read much. Well, because I don't get a chance. But I really like books. I'm sure I'd like your books." Nick realized he was digging himself into a hole. "But come to think of it, my mother's a big fan of yours. She loves to read. Reading is important."

"That's what my publisher says," Nora said with a smile.

"Can I get you a cup of tea or coffee?" Maria asked Nora.

"No, thank you. This should just take a minute."

"Please sit down," Nick urged as Maria exited the room shaking her head.

"You have a lovely hotel," Nora began.

"Oh, thank you. We aim to please. Is everything okay with your room?"

"Oh, yes," Nora answered. "My husband and I are down here for the funeral convention."

"Really?" Nick tried to sound excited. "With his line of work, he must be able to give you a lot of plots for your books."

"He's got some good stories," Nora agreed.

"You know," Nick continued with enthusiasm,

"I've often wondered what it would be like to wake up in the funeral parlor, you know, before they started working on you." Nick laughed. "Would your family get their deposit back?"

Nora looked at him. "Well, I don't know. Everybody who's come through my husband's place has been dead on arrival."

"Right, right, right," Nick chuckled. "Maybe they'd just hit you with a pickup charge. Like I said, that had just occurred to me once or twice. I don't know why. Something to think about, I guess . . ." My God, he thought, I'm babbling, and it's only nine-fifteen in the morning.

"Well, what I'd like to talk about . . ." Nora began.

"Shoot," Nick laughed. "Of course I don't want you to really shoot me, it's just an expression I use . . ."

"I wouldn't dream of shooting you," Nora assured him, "except maybe in a book."

"That'd be great! Name one of your characters Nick and make him a handsome devil and I'll be sure to buy it."

"You've got a deal. Now what I wanted to ask you is about the availability of rooms for a cocktail party tomorrow afternoon."

Nick whistled and tried to look stern. He liked to do that when something big was happening. It made him feel important.

"I know it's late notice, but something has come up and it's rather important . . ."

Nick assumed the role of captain of the ship as he

pulled out his room chart and spread it out on the desk. "You know we have a lot going on this weekend and all my conference rooms and party rooms are booked, booked, booked. I don't know what to say . . ."

"That is a shame," Nora sighed. "And to think that Richie has all the models lined up . . ."

Nick's ears perked up faster than a dog's at the first sound of a howling coyote. He almost leaned his head against his shoulder and whimpered. He tried to sound calm as he asked, "What is the occasion for your party?"

"A friend of ours has a special panty hose he wants to show off. As a matter of fact, I'm wearing a pair right now . . ."

"They're lovely."

"Thank you. Oh—his niece is having her wedding reception here on Sunday. Maura Durkin."

"Of course. That's going to be a big one. They've ordered everything from soup to nuts. Now getting back to your party . . ."

"Oh, yes. Well, this friend, Richie Blossom, has this panty hose and he's asked several of the models from South Beach to be in an informal fashion show. We wanted to have a cocktail party for the panty-hose executives and the models beforehand, but I guess we'll have to figure something else out."

"Hmmmm." Nick didn't want to seem too anxious, but he could barely contain himself. "I hate to let you down, seeing as the family is having the wedding here. Now I've never done this before, but I'd really like to help you out. I live in a big penthouse suite upstairs, which is just perfect for parties. I'd be happy to let you use it. Of course I'll be on hand to help out.''

"That sounds like the best place of all to have a party!" Nora enthused.

"Oh, it is, it is! I've had some great parties myself up there. You'll love it. You know, you could have the fashion show up there too. We could build a little runway running the length of my living room, against the windows, looking out at the sea. It will enhance and glamorize your product, I'm sure of it.''

Nora seized the opportunity to take advantage of his zeal. "I was wondering . . . do you have a list of the panty-hose executives and which rooms they're staying in? I want to send them personal invitations.''

"Right here. Aren't you going to send the models invitations?''

"I don't think we have to," Nora said, "since they'll be in the fashion show.''

"Of course," Nick agreed heartily. With trembling hands he pulled out the computer printout of the panty-hose people with their names, titles and room numbers.

"This is wonderful," Nora said.

"Now what we can do," Nick pronounced, "is set up a bar in the dining room . . .''

In the next few minutes they agreed on an open bar and hors d'oeuvres with waiters serving.

"I'll give you a head count tomorrow morning," Nora concluded. "Thanks for all your help.''

As soon as she was out the door, Nick picked up

the phone to housekeeping. "Make sure my flowered print shirt is back from the valet by tomorrow morning." As he replaced the phone in its cradle, Nick's face settled into a frown. He knew he had a big decision to make.

REGAN AND RICHIE walked over to the Models Models Modeling Agency, located just a few blocks from the Fourth Quarter.

"Everything is so close to everything else around here," Regan commented.

"South Beach only takes up one square mile. That's why it's great for us old-timers. We can walk everywhere and we don't have to worry about the upkeep of a car," Richie replied.

As they climbed the stairs to the third-floor office, Regan's mind kept jumping in three different directions. I must call Maura, she thought. She said she was going to be out doing some errands this morning, but I bet she's home by now. I should see if she needs help with anything. I'd like to read over these articles about Dolly

Twiggs, even though it doesn't look like there's much there. But I don't want to leave Richie alone. Something told her trouble was brewing, and until the sale of the Fourth Quarter was settled, Regan had the uneasy feeling that he was not safe.

Inside the agency, two models sat on a bench and both greeted Richie by name. Elaine Bass sat behind a large metal desk. Pictures of models posing, running and frolicking covered every wall of the small office. Elaine's assistant, a young man named Scott, was stationed at a counter in the corner where he was sorting through pictures and answering phone calls. Bright sunlight streamed through the open windows.

As introductions were made, Regan took in Elaine's gruff yet appealing manner. She had a no-nonsense air about her that was necessary for her business. You couldn't be ultrasensitive when you had to turn away countless hopefuls—hopefuls who just didn't have the look that happened to be in style.

"Richie, you're doing great, honey," Elaine said. "We're really pleased about this commercial. And the client loves you." She turned to Regan. "We had every guy over sixty in Miami trying out for this part. Your friend here beat them all hands down."

"A couple of the guys at the Fourth Quarter tried out too," Richie said. "I was afraid to tell them I'd gotten the part."

"That's show biz, baby," Elaine said matter-of-factly. "Scott, get out Richie's check. Now, Richie, both Willow and Annabelle here are coming over to your place today for the rehearsal."

The girls smiled at Richie.

Elaine continued. "They can only stay for an hour. No overtime. Now that's a laugh, they're not even getting paid." She turned to Regan. "I don't know how he talked me into this." She did not wait for a response. "My models usually get paid from the minute they set foot on a shoot."

"Richie's got that way about him," Regan laughed.

"Yeah, right. Well, if he hadn't given me a pair of these panty hose,"—Elaine pulled out her leg from behind the desk—"I wouldn't have known how great they are. Listen, we're ordering up some sandwiches. You two want to join us for lunch? There's a photographer coming up in about an hour and I want him to take a look at you, Richie. I think you'd be right for a project he's got going."

Regan looked at her watch. It was just about noon. "Richie, I'd like to go back to my hotel to make a few phone calls. How about if I come back and get you at about one-thirty?"

"You don't have to come back and get me, Regan," Richie protested. "Don't you want to go to the beach?"

"She knows it's not a good idea to sit in the hot sun at this time of day," Elaine interjected. "I tell all my girls that. That doesn't mean they always listen."

Regan laughed. "I've never been to a rehearsal for a fashion show before. I don't want to miss it. I'll come get you and we'll head back to your place."

"Good enough," Richie said. "Elaine, I'll have a pastrami on rye . . ."

BACK IN HER hotel room, Regan immediately turned on the air conditioner. It was definitely getting hot and muggy. She poured herself a glass of water, plopped down on the bed, and called Maura.

"How's it going?" Regan asked when Maura answered.

"Well, I had a trial run this morning with a hairdresser to see what he'd do. I thought banana curls went out twenty years ago."

"I didn't know they were ever in."

"I think I'm going to go out back and jump in the pool. John's coming over in a little while and I don't want him to see me looking like this. It's not too late for him to back out."

"Maybe he has a fondness for banana curls," Regan

said. "They might remind him of a girl he had a crush on in the first grade."

"This is not the time to remind him of old girl-friends," Maura said dryly. "How are things with you?"

"I was with Richie this morning," Regan said. "I was a little bit concerned about him."

"I don't like what happened last night either," Maura said. "And he's so worried about losing that place. Your mother's so nice to help him out with the cocktail party tomorrow."

"I have to call her to see how that's going. I wanted to help Richie with his fashion-show rehearsal this afternoon if you didn't need me for anything."

"That'd be great, Regan. I'd appreciate it if you stayed with Richie. We'll all be getting together tonight, anyway. This afternoon I'll be bringing my tresses to a new salon to see what style they dream up. Maybe I'll end up with a Mohawk."

"Have them dye half of it purple," Regan suggested.

"To match my mother's dress," Maura replied. "Anyway, I'll see you guys tonight at the Watergreen." Maura paused. "Watch out for Richie."

"I will," Regan said, trying to keep her tone light. When she hung up the phone, she felt uneasy as she opened the file on her bed. "And now for a look at Dolly Twiggs."

NEARLY AN HOUR had passed since Nora had sat down at the desk in her room and started writing out the envelopes with the names of the panty-hose executives who were being invited to the cocktail party. There wasn't time for fancy invitations. Nora had drafted an invitation which Maria had offered to type up and run off on her computer. "I'll even fool around with the graphics and see what I can do to make it look special," she had said. As soon as they were ready, Maria was going to send them up to the room.

Nora took a sip of the cranberry juice she'd taken from the minibar. It was nearly noon. As soon as I finish this last envelope, I wouldn't mind having lunch by the pool, she thought.

Behind her, the door opened and Nora whirled around. Luke smiled at her.

"How did it go, dear?" Nora asked.

"There was a little mixup with which room the coffins go in, but once we got that squared away, everything was fine. We're all registered and now I'm free for a couple of hours." He took off his jacket. "Have you had a relaxing morning?"

"Relaxing, not really. Fruitful, yes. I've spent the whole time arranging Richie's cocktail party. All the party rooms in the hotel were booked, so the manager offered to have it in his penthouse suite. He's an awfully nice young fellow. Maybe Regan would like him . . ."

"She'll kill you," Luke said matter-of-factly.

"Oh, I know. It's just that he's being so nice and helpful. I really hope this party helps Richie out with the panty hose. It would be such a shame if Richie and his friends lost their place."

Luke nodded. "Stick to worthy causes like that. Not matchmaking, it never works."

"Are you forgetting, dear, that we met on a blind date?"

"That was different. First of all, it wasn't arranged by your mother . . ."

The doorbell rang.

Luke looked at Nora quizzically. "Did you order room service?"

"Are you kidding? I want to go down and eat poolside if you don't mind."

"I'll be your date," Luke said as he went over and opened the door.

Nick Fargus stood in front of him with a stack of folded papers in his hand. "Are you Mr. Reilly?"

"Yes, I am."

"Nick Fargus." He shook Luke's hand. "I'm the manager of the Watergreen and we're just trying to help your wife arrange a little party for tomorrow."

"Come in, Nick," Nora called.

"I've got the invitations here. They're all ready to go."

"How sweet of you," Nora said. "I just have to stuff them into the envelopes and stick them under the doors."

"Oh, no, we'll take care of that," Nick said firmly, assuming his captain's tone. He handed Nora an invitation. "Does this look satisfactory to you?"

Nora looked at it and smiled at the sketches of pantyhose-clad legs surrounding the border. "Luke, listen to this:

> "Don't be kept in suspense any longer. Nora Regan Reilly invites you to join her for cocktails, hors d'oeuvres, and the unveiling of panty hose you could die for.
> Don't hit a snag!
> Run to Penthouse A at three o'clock Saturday afternoon and you'll never have to get a run in your stockings again."

Nora took off her reading glasses and looked up. "What do you think, Luke?"

"I'd come."

"I appreciate your vote of confidence."

Nick laughed. "Well, I guess we're all set, then. I'll get these right out. Mr. Reilly, I know you're here for the funeral convention. Has everything met with your satisfaction?"

"Oh, sure. We had a little problem this morning with getting the coffins in and where they were to be displayed, but it's all straightened out now. I guess there was a mixup with the rooms."

Nick laughed nervously. "Oh, yes, I got a call about that this morning. We almost ended up with mannequins in their panty hose in the same room as the coffins. Now that would have been interesting. If we had laid them down in the coffins, it would have given new meaning to the term 'good-looking stiff.' " Beads of sweat broke out on his brow. Oh, my God, Nick thought, I can't believe I said that.

Luke looked at him. "I suppose it would have."

"Well, I guess I'd better get going. We want to get these out." Nora handed him the envelopes. Nick shook the invitations in the air and hurried out of the room.

Luke looked at Nora incredulously. "So that's what you're looking for in a son-in-law?"

Nora looked squeamish. "He means well."

Luke smiled. "Famous last words." He stretched out his arms. "I'm going to get changed. Then let's go downstairs, grab seats at the floating bar in the pool, and try one of the piña coladas this place is so famous for."

NADINE LAY SPRAWLED on the beach, covered head to toe with suntan lotion. This is great, she thought. But it's getting a little hot.

She got up from her towel and walked to the water's edge where the surf lapped up against her feet as they sank in the sand. It wasn't too cold, but Nadine, never one to endure unnecessary discomfort, didn't like the slow torture of getting used to water that was any cooler than the air. Impulsively she ran and dived in, enjoying the sensation of spiraling underwater, being cut off from all sound except for the muffled hum you hear on those boring shows about marine life they film underwater.

When Nadine surfaced, she threw back her hair and dived again in an attempt to catch a wave. She slowly rode it in and got up and dived again. Her hands hit the bottom, her fingers scraping the tiny shells and pebbles.

"Damn it!" Nadine said and swallowed a gulp of water. She got on her feet and examined the damage. Three of her precious nails broken. "This gets me really aggravated," she muttered as she walked out of the water and up to her towel. "It's a gorgeous day and I gotta go get my nails done."

Nadine picked up her belongings and headed back to Joey's house. She stopped at the faucet at the edge of the beach and got in line to rinse off her feet. While she stood there waiting for some kid who obviously felt he had to remove every grain of sand from his lower limbs, Nadine watched a model a few feet away posing for a photographer as an assistant held up a reflector. The model was wearing a winter coat. You'd have to pay me a lot of money to stand around and sweat, Nadine thought. And even more to put up with a photographer who sounds like he has PMS. What language was he barking at her in anyway? Swedish?

Finally getting her turn, Nadine rinsed off and slipped on her sandals. Crossing the street, Nadine tried to figure where she should go for her nail repair. Maybe I'll get in Joey's car and go for a little ride, she thought. There has to be a mall around here somewhere.

DISGUSTED, REGAN THREW down the papers on her bed. There was nothing in them that would help. Dolly Twiggs was a well-liked woman. She and her husband had bought the apartment building for a song forty years ago. When her husband died, Dolly took over the care of the place, but toward the end of her life she'd been anxious to sell it. She had no children. She was survived by her sister, Lucille Coyle, who also had no children.

Her body had been discovered by a group of early risers who made a ritual of their morning swim. One of them, Sid Bernstein, was quoted as saying, "We were all shocked when we came down to the beach and saw her there. I just wish we could have caught the guy who did this. I had been to some of the socials at the Fourth

Quarter. Dolly was a very giving person. She had told me that as soon as an apartment became available there, she'd get me in.''

An unidentified woman had said, ''This place has become a crazy combination of haves and have-nots. On the one hand you've got the people with all their money and glitz. And on the other you have the homeless and the transients who have nothing. You've got the drug-taking going on in the clubs and the whiskey-drinking in the alleys. And Dolly Twiggs, a decent, churchgoing woman who lived here for years before anybody even heard of this place, can't even walk the beach. I wouldn't put it past anybody I see around here to have done this.''

Great, Regan thought. The entire population is suspect. If it weren't for the fact we were almost run down last night, I could probably accept this as being another crime motivated by the desire for instant money. But something tells me there's more to the story.

Regan picked up her phone and dialed her parents. She let it ring four times before the operator came back on and asked if she'd like to leave a message.

''Yes,'' Regan said. ''Tell them their daughter is calling and I'll see them tonight.''

''Your name?'' the operator asked efficiently.

I think they know it, Regan thought, but said, ''Nancy Drew.''

''Thank you, Nancy. Have a good day.''

''You too.'' The second Regan hung up the phone, it started to ring. She picked it up.

''Hello.''

"Is this Regan Reilly?" the male voice at the other end said.

"Yes, it is. Who is this?"

"My name is Henry. I'm the waiter from the café where you nearly got run over last night."

"Oh, yes, hi."

"I thought you might be interested in knowing that I was over on Collins Avenue today. A tow-truck driver was hitching a car up that reminded me of the one that went by so fast last night. Well, I'll admit it, I'm nosy, so I went over and asked him why he was taking it away."

"What did he say?" Regan asked quickly.

"Are you ready for this?" Henry asked rhetorically.

"I'm ready." More than ready, she thought.

"It was a stolen vehicle."

A SCREAM PIERCED the air in the Calla-Lily suite. "I can't believe this! What did I tell you?" Ruth shouted.

Ethel stood dutifully by her side as Ruth read the invitation from Nora Regan Reilly.

"Now everybody will go to this cocktail party and take a closer look at the panty hose; won't they, Ethel?"

Ethel shook her head mournfully for the umpteenth time that day, then asked hesitantly, "Well, if you go, would you mind getting her to sign a book for me?"

"SHUT UP!" Ruth charged over to the desk and plunked down her purse. "Have we heard from the mule trek?"

"No. But we did get some good news," Ethel offered cheerfully. "Bradford Stempler the Third was sighted in the Canary Islands and is on his way back. They're still trying to locate Preston Landers.''

"I'm glad everybody else has time for vacations. I don't suppose Irving has checked in.''

"No, ma'am.''

Ruth picked up the phone and dialed the lab. After six rings, Irving finally answered.

"Yes.''

"What's going on?'' Ruth demanded.

"Hello, Ruth.''

"Is there anything new to tell me?''

Irving sighed. "This stuff is like kryptonite. It just won't destruct. These panty hose could bring down the whole industry. Just like computers have practically made typewriters obsolete—''

"Don't rub it in! How many more tests do you have to do?''

"A few. I gave another pair to my mother-in-law this morning. She will be running all over town today and is also in a bad mood, so maybe she'll manage to wear them down.''

"Irving, we have got to get the patent on this.''

"What about when the patent expires?''

"That wouldn't be for another seventeen years!''

"What then, Ruth?'' Irving asked mildly. "But I guess you won't have to worry. By then you'll be able to park yourself on that hammock in your backyard without feeling too guilty.''

"Not so, Irving! Grandpa stayed involved right until the end and I intend to do the same. Right before this patent expires we'll release these panty hose on the market. At least we'll get a jump on everybody else. And hopefully by then the fashion industry will have deemed it stylish to wear panty hose in twenty-two different colors.''

"In the next seventeen years I'm sure you'll have figured out a way to make that happen. You always manage to keep in control, Ruthie.'' Irving smiled at the other end of the phone. ''Well, not always.''

Ruth squirmed in her chair. "I've got to go. Keep me posted.'' Ruth hung up the phone and called out, "Ethel, we have to hire more helicopters. We're going to find that Davy Crockett Wannabe if it kills me!''

NADINE GOT IN Joey's car and flinched when her bare legs hit the burning-hot seat. "Let's get some air-conditioning going here," she mumbled as she started the car and flipped the temperature control to full blast. As even hotter air came spewing out, Nadine cupped her hands underneath her thighs to keep them from sticking to the vinyl interior. "Hurry up, cold air, hurry up."

When she came back to the house she had showered and changed into a pair of shorts and a T-shirt. It was so nice to be in Joey's house, around his things, even though he and his roommates kept it a mess. There was something endearing about all the guy stuff all over the place. Barbells and a rowing machine in the living room surrounded by mismatched furniture that looked as if it had been picked off the streets after three days of rain. Faded curtains with uneven hemlines that were probably already old when Ponce de León discovered Florida. Sneakers and sweatshirts and gym bags and golf balls left wherever they happened to land on the once-yellow carpeting, and it didn't seem to bother them one bit. She had been tempted to start cleaning up but decided to forget it, remembering the earthy wisdom of her grandmother, "If a guy has a messy apartment, he's just your typical bachelor. But if a girl has a messy apartment, she's branded a slob."

Backing out of the driveway, Nadine thought that she could really get used to Miami. Now we just have to get Joey used to the idea of together forever. This cross-country commuting was getting to be too much, not to mention the effect flying was having on her sinuses. She hated the empty unsettled feeling she got when she headed back after these long weekends. Joseph, she thought, when are you going to buy me just a one-way ticket here?

Nadine drove along the busy two-lane road, lost in her thoughts. Suddenly she came upon a huge sign that said: GRAND OPENING—NAIL SALON. Quickly she glanced in the rearview mirror and decided she had time to make a quick turn into the driveway. She pulled into a parking space right in front. If it's a grand opening, she thought, then they'll want to do a decent job and make sure people come back. They don't have to know I'm not a resident of Miami. At least, not yet.

AFTER REGAN HAD picked up Richie at the agency, they sauntered up Ocean Drive, back to the Fourth Quarter. Once inside, they headed upstairs to Richie's apartment to gather the panty hose for the rehearsal. The message light on Richie's answering machine was blinking.

"It's always nice to come home and see that someone has left a message, isn't it, Regan?"

"Yeah, except when you play it back and it's a hangup."

Richie pushed the playback button and an electronic voice that always sounded flat, no matter how many people had called, said, "Number of messages received—one." Somehow Regan thought the voice should sound more and more excited the higher the number got. Or maybe it should say something like: "Congratulations—you had eight people call." Or: "You must be *really* popular—twelve messages." Or: "Do you have a lot of overdue bills?—twenty-three messages."

A moment later, Nora Regan Reilly's message began. "Richie, this is Nora. I've got great news. We have a suite upstairs that we can use for the cocktail party and the fashion show. Give me a call."

"Your mother's a saint," Richie said breathlessly as he hurriedly dialed the Watergreen, "an absolute saint."

"Saint Nora," Regan said. "It has a nice ring to it. Maybe they should put her books in the religious section."

"Hello, Nora," Richie's voice boomed. "How are you, love?"

Regan watched Richie's face light up as her mother started to give him the details about the party. "Wait a minute, Nora, let me put you on the speakerphone. Regan's right here."

"Hi, Mom," Regan called out.

"Hi, Nancy," Nora said.

Regan smiled. "You got my message."

"Yes, dear. The clerk at the front desk asked me if I liked to carry the mystery theme through everything in life."

"Tell 'em you have a son at home named Edgar Allan Poe Reilly."

"Hey, Nora," Richie said excitedly, "tell Regan about what you told me about the arrangements . . ."

"The manager here is a lovely young man . . ." Nora began and for the next ten minutes they discussed how everything would work on Saturday. They finally hung up, saying they'd see each other later at the Watergreen for dinner with the Durkins.

"Richie," Regan said, "have you got any music planned for this fashion show?"

"Music?" Richie asked with a startled expression. "I never thought of that."

"It helps to set a mood, create excitement. Designers always have music at their shows. Do you have a stereo?"

Richie looked at her guiltily. "Well . . ." He led her over to an orange Victrola with a picture of a bewildered-looking brown-and-white dog sniffing at a horn. The label said, "His Master's Voice."

Regan stared at it. "I don't think this is going to work." She could just picture herself cranking this thing while the models from the agency strutted their stuff down the runway. "But you do have a collector's item here, I will say that."

Richie's eyes moistened. "Birdie and I bought it when we were first married. We used to love to turn it on and dance. We had taken dancing lessons before we got married so we wouldn't look like jerks when we got out on the floor."

"I think Maura and John have been taking a crash course this past week," Regan said. "Well, let's not worry about the music right now. We've got to get downstairs, they'll all be here. I'll call my mother later and see if that 'lovely young man' has a stereo in his suite that we can use. Now, let's get out that panty hose . . .''

"You're a saint too, Regan, you know that?"

"Richie, please, you don't have to go that far. My mother? Maybe. Me? I know I'm not a saint," Regan laughed.

"Well, then you're my guardian angel."

Regan's blood chilled. After what happened last night, it didn't sound like such a joke.

NADINE STEPPED INSIDE the red-, white- and blue-streamered doorway of the Hard As Nails nail salon and shivered. Ice-cold air was spewing from an air conditioner in the corner as a workman stood on a ladder trying to fix it. She was immediately greeted by a zealous aesthetician with jet-black hair and lots of makeup, whom Nadine guessed to be in her late forties.

"You'd like a manicure and a pedicure?"

Nadine rubbed her arms. "It's cold in here."

"We're fixing it right away. You'd like a manicure and a pedicure?" she repeated hopefully.

"Do you sterilize your instruments?" Nadine asked prudently.

"Yes, of course. We have the special sterilizing machine. It cooks the germs real good."

"Okay then." Nadine agreed to stay even though she was the only customer in sight, always a cause for wonder. But, Nadine reasoned, it was the grand opening and maybe they needed a little time to get cooking on all four burners. Everything certainly looked ready to go. Six manicure stations were set up in the tiny storefront. Magazines were piled on a bamboo table in the reception area, which presumably on busy days would be filled with clients with ragged cuticles and chipped polish, awaiting their turn side by side with others sporting tissue paper between their splayed toes, impatiently waiting for that magic moment when their nails were pronounced dry and it was safe to put their shoes back on.

"I'm Sophia," the woman said to Nadine. "Come sit down. I'll get a nice tub of hot water for your feet."

"I don't want a pedicure," Nadine said firmly. "I just need to have new tips put on these fingernails."

"We specialize in tips," Sophia enthused, masking her disappointment. "Next time you'll have a pedicure." It sounded like an order.

Nadine sat down at Sophia's station, listening to her explanation that a couple of her girls weren't starting until tomorrow, one had called in sick on her first day—can you believe it?—and she still had to hire a few more, but only the best.

Hurry up, Nadine thought. Get to work.

Sophia took Nadine's afflicted hand in hers and studied it. "You did some good job breaking these nails. They look awful." Then she added reassuringly, "Don't worry, I fix."

As Sophia diligently worked, interrupted by an occasional "Ow, be careful" from Nadine, Nadine watched the air-conditioning guy go up and down the ladder several times to rummage through his toolbox. He's cute, Nadine thought. But not as cute as Joey.

Suddenly the door to the salon was flung open.

"Can I get a manicure?" a robust elderly woman shouted. "I got one of your coupons in the mail."

Sophia dropped Nadine's hand and rushed over. "Of course, of course. One more minute."

The woman turned and yelled to someone waiting in a car. "You can go now. They'll take me. Come back soon, though. I don't want to sit around here all day."

"Come in, come in," Sophia twittered. "One more minute."

You said that a minute ago, Nadine thought.

Sophia's newest customer unloaded herself into the seat next to Nadine. "It's cold in here," she complained.

Nadine noticed the repairman throwing her a dirty look.

"The air conditioner is working too hard," Sophia joked. "We're fixing it right away, right away."

The woman looked at Nadine's bare legs. "Aren't you cold?"

"Freezing," Nadine said.

"Thank God I have my panty hose on. Otherwise I'd leave right now."

Nadine wrinkled her nose. "Isn't it a hot day to wear panty hose?"

"These are different," the woman announced with

authority. She lifted up her long housedress to reveal a beautiful pair of pink hose. "They breathe. They keep you cool when you want to be cool and warm when you want to be warm. And the best part is they don't run or snag."

"You've got to be kidding me," Nadine said as she stared at the woman's legs.

"Not at all. I didn't believe it either until I tried them myself."

"Where did you get them?" Nadine asked incredulously.

The woman let go of her dress and lowered her voice. "They're not out yet. My son-in-law is an engineer. He's testing them for his company to make sure they're for real. They want to buy the rights to them. It's some big hush-hush thing. He doesn't say much about it. As a matter of fact, he doesn't say much at all."

"All done!" Sophia blurted as she screwed the cap onto the nail polish bottle. "Be careful."

"I know," Nadine said. She leaned down for her purse at the same moment the panty-hose-clad woman started to get up from her seat.

"Oh, no!" Nadine wailed as her wet nails grazed the woman's legs and smeared. "My nails are ruined." After a pause she added, "And so are your panty hose."

"No problem with them," the woman said and wiped the bright-red polish off her leg.

Nadine was awed. "That's incredible," she said. "Nail polish is what you use to stop a run. It never comes off."

"I told you," the woman said, "these panty hose are

different. My only question is why did they have to wait until I'm this old before they discovered them?''

As Sophia reapplied polish to Nadine's twice-damaged nails, Nadine and the older woman exchanged addresses.

''As soon as those panty hose go on sale you've got to let me know,'' Nadine said. ''Have you ever tried to buy sheer black panty hose late on a Saturday afternoon during the holidays? The hosiery counter is a nightmare. I'll buy these in every color and never have to shop for them again!''

''Me too,'' Sophia insisted as she plopped down a bowl of hot soapy water into which she plunged the septuagenarian's unsuspecting fingertips.

REGAN AND RICHIE hurried as they set up the folding chairs in the Dolly Twiggs Memorial Room. It was a quarter of three and the models, young and old, were expected at three o'clock.

"This works out great," Richie said as he unfolded the last chair. "We'll be all ready for the memorial service at four."

"Why didn't you just leave the chairs set up after your meeting yesterday?" Regan asked.

"House rules," Richie said. "Or should I say, Flo rules. She thinks the place looks like a church basement when these things are set up. Takes away the homey look. She said if we didn't make a strict policy, then they'd never get put away."

Regan looked around. The spacious room was furnished with three floral couches and several armchairs, all arranged so they had a good view of the television set.

"Do people come down here at night to watch TV?" Regan asked.

"Day and night," Richie answered. "Most of the time you'll find someone in here watching something. The only time it gets real crowded and we have to haul out the folding chairs is when there's a program on that no one likes to watch alone, you know, like disaster reports, or the Super Bowl, or"—Richie chuckled—"when the President decides to talk to the nation. We get everyone in here heckling and shouting at the TV on those nights. Yeah, that's one tough job. Must be hard to live knowing there's always somebody out to get you."

"Hi, Richie." The two young models whom Regan had met at the agency appeared in the doorway.

"Hi ya, hi ya, how you doing, come on in," Richie urged.

By five past three, all the other models had filtered in. Fifteen residents of the Fourth Quarter, along with the five models sent over by Elaine at the agency, made up the cast.

Greetings were exchanged, and finally Richie said, "Ladies, ladies, please sit down. We have a lot to do and not that much time."

As they settled themselves in, Richie waited for absolute silence. He cleared his throat. "Tomorrow is going to be a very important and exciting day, not only for those of us who call the Fourth Quarter our home, but also in the history of panty hose.''

"We hope,'' Bessie Tibbens, who lived down the hall from Richie, yelled.

"You said it!'' shouted another.

"Your lips to God's ear,'' Flo pronounced as she circled the room with her tray of cookies, offering one to a young model sitting there crunching on a carrot stick.

"No, thank you. I never touch sweets,'' she purred.

"I'm sure glad I got old before they started pushing that rabbit food on us. A couple of cookies a day never hurt anybody.'' Flo moved along with her tray, only to have the next young model decline her offer with a shake of her head and a wave of her Evian bottle. "Land's sakes,'' Flo mumbled.

"Flo, please sit down,'' Richie pleaded.

"I am, I am.''

"Tomorrow,'' Richie continued, "is a day I liken to the day when man walked on the moon. Instead of 'One small step for man, one giant leap for mankind,' it will be 'One small step in the Birdie Panty Hose, one giant leap for womankind.' ''

"July 20, 1969,'' Pearl Schwartz recalled, uninvited. "My little grandkids had just gotten halfway through lighting the candles on my birthday cake when that guy finally decided to come out of his spaceship. So they blew them out and then, after he'd bounced around for a few minutes up there, they relit them. The cake turned out to be a waxy mess. By the time I peeled all the wax off my piece, half the icing was gone.''

"You should have had a cheesecake in honor of the occasion," Flo offered.

"Pearl, Flo, please, we'll have time for chatting later," Richie moaned. "Now, as I was saying, tomorrow could be the beginning of a new era for women. To wear comfortable, flattering panty hose that doesn't run or snag, that dries in about thirty seconds, that doesn't bag around your ankles in embarrassing folds. This is what we will be revealing to the world tomorrow. I need you to help create the excitement." Richie looked to the young models seated together. "That's what fashion shows are all about, right, girls?"

They nodded their heads almost imperceptibly.

"Right," Richie said as if to answer himself. "What we have here is a great product, so it shouldn't be too difficult to get people interested in it. I hope. Hell's bells, when you think of some of the stuff they try to pass off at those fancy-schmancy fashion shows—those clothes look like they were designed by someone on Pluto. But people buy them even though their price tag is in outer orbit too. So why shouldn't a panty-hose company want to buy my invention?"

"Don't say hell, Richie," Flo admonished.

"Sorry. Now before I get started, I want to thank the models from the agency who came out to lend us a hand. They're donating their time to help us save our home." Richie started to clap and was soon joined by the rest of the group in a round of polite applause.

"And right next to me here . . ."

Oh God, Regan thought.

". . . is my friend Regan Reilly. She's here to help me out. Stand up, Regan."

Regan stood up, smiled, waved, then sat back down. Quickly. That has to be one of the more awkward rituals that human beings subject themselves to, she thought. The introduction to a big group. And having to wave. It made her feel sorry for the Queen and beauty-pageant winners, who probably wave in their sleep.

"Regan's going to arrange for us to have some nice music during the show tomorrow."

Feeble applause started in the back of the room, and before Regan knew it, she was smiling and waving again.

"Regan's mother, Nora Regan Reilly, has arranged a cocktail party in one of the penthouse suites at the Watergreen. That's where we'll have the show, too. They're setting up a runway for us."

One of the women in the front row smiled sweetly at Regan. Regan smiled back.

The woman leaned forward in her chair. "Are you married, dear?"

"No."

"I have a grandson who has a nice little business going for himself . . ."

"Minnie, please," Richie said with frustration. "We've got a lot to get done."

Regan found herself propelled out of her chair by the force of her nerve endings. "Richie, why don't we distribute the panty hose?"

"Good thinking."

The twenty pairs of different-colored panty hose were handed out after much discussion about who should wear which color, who had a dress to match a certain shade of peach, violet, ivory, rust, et cetera.

"Remember," Richie said, "you have to wear dresses short enough so we can see your legs at least up to the knees. Some of you might want to go shorter."

"Oh, sure," Minnie mumbled.

Respectfully, Richie left the room as they all struggled into their assigned hose, amid murmurs of "These really do feel nice," and "How pretty."

Finally Regan called Richie back in.

"Birdie would be proud of you, Richie," Bessie called out. "These make my legs feel good."

"Thanks, Bessie."

Regan and Richie placed all twenty models in a line, with lovely Annabelle from the agency leading the pack.

"Annabelle," Richie said, "let's see how you walk across the room and back, like you do when you're in a show."

With a self-assured attitude, Annabelle strode the length of the Dolly Twiggs room, turned from side to side, paused, and then sauntered back with one hand on her hip and the other flowing at her side.

"That was great," Richie exulted. "Now, did you see what she did, everybody? That strut, that look in her eye, that pause at the end of the imaginary runway. You all do that and we'll have the audience eating out of the palms of your hands."

"I feel ridiculous trying that at my age," Pearl kvetched.

"Do you want to go back to living with your daughter-in-law?" Flo asked her.

"Of course not."

"Then get out there and strut."

"Oh, all right. I'll imagine I'm at one of the USO dances during the war."

Pearl started to shuffle across the floor.

"You have to look happy, Pearl," Richie advised.

"I'm trying, I'm trying."

"Well, pick up your head and stretch out your torso like Annabelle did."

"Like Annabelle! She's two feet taller than me to start with!"

"It's all in your attitude," Richie insisted. "I want to show that women at any age will look great in and will love Birdie Panty Hose."

They rehearsed with Pearl several times and before too long they had her swinging her arms and cracking a smile. "This is good exercise," she said.

"Tomorrow, when we have music, you can really get into the rhythm," Richie declared.

The other models each took their turns at parading across the room, listening to Richie's instructions to "be natural," and "flirt with the audience."

"Now that wasn't so bad," Richie said when they were all finished.

"The show really won't last that long, will it, Richie?" Regan asked.

"No, but that's good. People's attention spans are getting shorter by the minute. Your mother is going to narrate a little script she's writing. We just want to grab them, hook them, and let the bidding begin!"

One of the old girls raised her fist. "Let's do it!"

"What about some sort of finale?" Regan asked. "Something to pull it all together at the end."

"Like the Rockettes!" Richie exclaimed.

"Well, something like that."

The models lined up side by side with their arms around each other's waists, and at Richie's repeated urgings, kicked up their heels. Slightly.

"Come on, a little more, a little more. Just look like you're having fun. At the end of the song you'll all file off the runway, snapping your fingertips. We want to bring the house down with this number."

"You're going to end up bringing me down," Pearl said. "If I kick too high, I'll lose my balance."

"Do what you can, Pearl," Richie advised. He turned to Regan. "Can you think of anything else we should cover before the group breaks up?"

"Richie, we want to get started with the memorial service," a voice said. Regan turned to see Elmer Pickett standing in the doorway.

"Have a chocolate cookie, Elmer," Flo snapped. "I can assure you, there are plenty left."

He's such a disagreeable soul, Regan thought.

"A couple more minutes, Elmer," Richie said and turned to the young models, who were now anxious to hurry off to other appointments. "If everyone could just leave their panty hose in one of the plastic bags and mark your name on it, I'd appreciate it. We'll have a changing room in the suite. Get there early tomorrow, everyone, and we'll knock 'em dead!''

If someone doesn't get to us first, Regan thought.

H E SAT IN the phone booth and sighed, twirling his finger around the cord. The crackling noise in his ear was finally joined by the sound of a foreign ring. The long-distance connection to South America was finally going through.

The phone was answered by a man with a heavily accented voice.

He let go of the cord and nervously identified himself.

"Well, what's going on?" the voice asked.

"We haven't been able to get him yet."

"Why not?" the man with the accent asked angrily.

"All day today he's been with that girl."

"So, get rid of her too! Don't you realize that we're running out of time?"

"I know. Don't worry. One way or another it'll get done."

"It better get done. There's a lot at stake here. I knew we should have started this sooner, but you . . ." The man took a deep breath. "You said there wouldn't be a problem."

"I didn't think there would be. And there still might not be."

"I don't want to hear any excuses or explanations. Get it done!" The phone clicked.

He sat there holding the receiver in his hand. "It will be," he said after a moment, slamming the phone back down and pulling open the door. "You can be sure it will be."

F I SHALL walk through the valley of death, I shall
have no fear. I know that my sister, Dolly, will be
there to greet me and we can go on that walk on the
beach in heaven together.'' Lucille, with tear-filled
eyes, looked around the congregation gathered in the
Dolly Twiggs Memorial Room. ''My sister was so fond
of you all. I feel she's looking down right now and
sending a spiritual greeting. But I know she would have
wanted you all to have something physical to remember
her by, something that was important to her. There's a
box of her seashells by the door. Please take one on
your way out.''

A hum of gratitude rippled through the audience.

''I know that she also would have wanted you to raise
the money to buy the Fourth Quarter and live here for

the duration of your earthly lives. I want that too. More than anything. So let us join hands and pray silently, in the religion of our choice, for the sale of Richie's panty hose.''

Regan and Richie joined hands. Regan turned to Elmer Pickett, who was sitting on her other side. He was sitting there with his arms folded. Clearly he did not intend to hold hands with anybody.

For someone who wanted to get this service started on time, Regan thought, he certainly doesn't seem to be fully participating in the tribute. Or was it the sale of the panty hose that he didn't want to pray for?

Regan looked around at the rest of the group. Everyone else's eyes were closed, some shut so tightly it looked as they were squinting in the desert sun, as if the harder they squeezed, the more likely the panty hose would generate some cash.

''Amen,'' Lucille finally said.

''Amen.''

''Amen.''

''Amen.''

Up and down the rows of folding chairs the word was heard.

Lucille quietly took her seat in the front row.

Flo, who Regan figured must have been president of the pep club in high school, got up and addressed the group.

''When Dolly died, with the way she died, on the beach, alone, we were all in shock. We had a funeral but we never really came together to talk about Dolly and honor her until now. Time is a healer, thank God, and today we want to celebrate her life with joy. This was a woman who kept our rents low all through the years. She wanted to keep us together as long as possible. When she could no longer afford to keep up this place, she promised us the chance to try and buy it for ourselves. This at a time when the prices around here started to skyrocket and she could have gotten way more than she was asking us. And now her sister, Lucille, who never really knew any of us before, has been so patient and is praying with us here so that we can raise the money to buy the Fourth Quarter. She isn't looking for a fortune, either. She just wants to get back to her gentleman friend in Texas.''

Lucille blushed. ''Flo, hush.''

''It's all right, Lucille. Now I invite anyone who would like to come up here and share. Share with us a story about Dolly, anything you'd like, about how she touched your life in some way.''

To Regan's surprise, Elmer Pickett got out of his seat and walked to the front of the room.

''I only moved in here shortly before Dolly died, but she was very welcoming to me,'' Elmer said almost accusingly to the other residents of the Fourth Quarter. ''My wife had just died and I didn't want to live all alone in our house. So I sold it and got an apartment here. Dolly was always there to talk to me when I was just moping around. One day we took a walk down the street outside here and saw all of those models getting their picture taken. They asked us to stop and be in the background. After that, Dolly encouraged me to try and get involved in the modeling. That's when I got an agent. I used to report back to Dolly about all the goings-on at the agency. She told me I should stop by there every day to see, maybe a call would come in when I was there and they'd need an old guy. It got me back on my feet again. Heck, I'm not a star, but it gave me a reason to get out of bed in the morning.''

Regan thought he directed his attention to Richie.

"I haven't gotten as much work lately, but whatever I do get, I have Dolly to thank for it.''

He's mad at Richie, Regan thought, for getting that commercial.

Next up was Pearl. "Every year on my birthday, which was the day the men landed on the moon, Dolly always baked me a special cake and stuck an American flag in it.'' Her voice quivered. "I'll always remember that.''

Minnie Kimble ambled out of her chair and recounted how she and Dolly used to love to walk on the beach together.

"Dolly was always picking up every seashell she passed and inspecting it to see if it was worth keeping. I used to say to her, 'Dolly, when are you going to stop collecting those shells? Haven't you got enough?' And she said her favorite tongue twister was 'She sells sea-shells by the seashore.' Try saying that three times fast.''

How about "The big black bug bled black blood,'' Regan thought.

Next up was Charlie Doonsday with his harmonica. "Before this area got busy with people wandering by all the time, Dolly and I used to sit outside on our beach chairs and I'd play my harmonica for her. Dolly, I hope you can hear this in heaven.'' He held the instrument up to his mouth and started to blow ''Home on the Range.''

The sea of humanity that passes outside on the sidewalk of South Beach doesn't leave much room for the deer and the antelope, Regan thought.

The duration of the hour-long service was filled with more personal stories, a few songs, and a tear-soaked rendition of ''Good-bye, Dolly.''

As they filed out, Regan checked her watch. It was ten past five.

''Richie, I'm going to go back and get changed for tonight. I'll pick you up at six-thirty. You'll be here, won't you?''

''Oh sure, Regan. I'll be here.''

I hope so, Regan thought as she hurried out the door.

REGAN STEPPED INTO the late-afternoon sun and glanced across the street at the ocean with its mildly breaking waves. At this time of day the beach looked peaceful. The setting sun's rays were reflecting off the water and most of the sunbathers had headed home.

Regan breathed in the salt air, turned and moseyed down the sidewalk, observing the cafés on the way to her hotel. It might be peaceful on the beach, she thought, but these joints are already getting crowded. Another night of mixing and mingling about to take off.

She reached a side street and waited at the curb for a spurt of traffic to pass before crossing. After last night, she wasn't about to take any chances. She had just stepped down into the street when she saw another car coming. In a reflex action she jumped back onto the curb and crashed into a rollerblader, who was knocked to the ground with her.

She felt a sharp pain as her elbow smashed into the ground. As she fell she saw his hand scrape along the sidewalk.

She heard him curse under his breath. "Watch it, would ya, lady?" he mumbled as he pulled himself up.

Anger flared in Regan as pain darted through her body. "Watch it yourself," she snapped as she struggled to her feet. "You shouldn't have been so close behind me."

He did not respond. He was already halfway down the side street, skating like lightning in his sunglasses and wide-brimmed straw hat.

Jerk, Regan thought. Her body felt sore all over. The jolt had shaken her badly. He was a solid guy. It was like hitting a brick wall.

She rubbed her elbow and looked around.

A middle-aged couple approached her. "Are you all right?" the man asked solicitously.

"Yes, thank you."

I backed into him, she thought. And he was moving forward. If he wanted to turn right down the side street, then he shouldn't have been so close to the curb where I was waiting. He would have just rounded the corner at the high speed he was traveling. Unless of course he *wanted* to be right behind me.

Once again Regan waited to cross the street and continued on to her hotel. Did he hurry off because he didn't want me to get a good look at him? she wondered. He looked like a geek with that hat. Was that a disguise? Was this related to last night?

Back in the hotel room, which more and more felt like her escape from the outside world, Regan kicked off her shoes and flopped on the bed. The ceiling fan was doing its thing and it made Regan think of New Orleans, even though she'd never been there. But her mind came back to the rollerblader. Who was he, and would he have pushed her into the street?

I need a bath, she thought. My bod could use a good soak. With the sore knee from last night and the bruise that was developing at that very moment, it was a good thing she was not in Richie's fashion show. Panty hose for the injured. Next thing you know I'll be wearing Ace bandages.

Two mishaps or accidents, or whatever one would call them, in twenty-four hours. And they say they come in threes. What's going to happen next? I'll probably slip in the tub, she decided. It would almost be a relief. Get it over with. She hadn't noticed any foot-shaped appliqués stuck on the bottom of the tub, the kind that were supposed to prevent you from a nasty spill. They were very tacky but practical. Whenever Regan saw them in a tub she imagined that they were the final footsteps of the Roto Rooter man who got lost in the drainpipes.

She went into the bathroom and turned on the faucets full blast. It sounded like Niagara Falls. Regan turned. Did she hear a sound in the bedroom? She always thought she was hearing things when the water was running.

Regan went back into the bedroom to check it out. Nothing. Everything was fine. Let's not get paranoid, she thought. She returned to the bathroom and shut the door. Peeling off her clothes, she gingerly stepped into the tub, feeling herself relax as the warm water enveloped her injuries. Using a towel as a pillow behind her, she lay back and closed her eyes. Within minutes she felt herself being drawn into a semiconscious state, that never-never land between sleep and wakefulness.

A few feet away the doorknob to the bathroom turned.

Regan's eyes sprang open and she jumped up and screamed. Dripping wet, she ran over and with her body barricaded the door. "Who's there? WHO'S THERE?" she screeched, her heart beating furiously.

"I'm sorry, miss," a meek woman's voice said. "Would you like some fresh towels?"

Regan exhaled sharply. "No, thank you, I'm fine."

"Would you like me to turn down your bed?"

"No, thank you, it's okay." Regan was starting to shiver.

"Would you like some chocolates for your pillow?"

Regan wanted to say "Yes, a box of Milk Duds," but resisted the urge. "No, thank you, I'm fine."

"Okay, miss, have a good evening then."

"Thank you, you too." So much for this place making me feel laid-back, Regan thought as she stepped back into the tub and slipped, grabbing the shower curtain. Two of the hooks snapped and the curtain went awry.

Three strikes, you're out, Regan thought miserably.

RICHIE PULLED ON his jacket and adjusted his tie. It was six-thirty. He picked up a bottle of the cologne from his dresser that he'd gotten from the holiday grab bag at the Fourth Quarter and sprayed it on. Normally he didn't like to wear cologne, but the ads for White Knight showed the guy who wore it to be a powerhouse driving a sexy car, with all the girls swooning over him. I wonder if it works with selling panty hose, Richie thought. He looked over at one of the many pictures of Birdie that adorned his apartment. "I don't want any swooners, honey. I just want to give off an aura in case I run into any of those panty-hose types at the hotel tonight."

In the mirror Richie studied his reflection and practiced a "Hello, I'm Richard Blossom. Yes, I am the inventor of the Birdie Panty Hose. I'd love to take a meeting.'' He paused. ''My agent?'' Richie frowned. He'd have to ask Regan about that one. He peered closer at himself. Is this the guy who's going to be a hero tomorrow? he wondered. Or is this the guy who's going to let down his friends?

Richie shrugged. Hey, fella, he thought, what happened to the power of positive thinking? That and a dollar might buy you an ice cream. They were getting so close. This was it. Either he made money on the panty hose this weekend, or the old gang was going to have to break up.

''Birdie,'' he said and picked up the picture of her wearing a French beret and standing in front of the Eiffel Tower under a drizzly sky. ''I need your help, honey.'' Briefly he got mad at her. ''If you hadn't died, I would never have moved in here and gotten so attached. And now we might lose it and I'll end up alone again.'' As Birdie stared back at him with her crooked smile, Richie felt ashamed. ''I'm sorry,'' he whispered. ''I guess our joke that we'd both keel over at the same old age from driving each other nuts was just a dream.'' He carefully replaced her picture on the antique oak dresser.

I've got to get moving, he thought. Regan's going to be here in a few minutes. He gathered up his wallet and ran a comb through the hair on the sides of his head. This'll be fun tonight. Little Maura getting married and I've hardly given it a thought. Well, if everything turns out, I'll get them an extra-special present.

The box of panty hose was by the front door. He glanced at it as he got out his keys and locked the door behind him. He'd wait outside on a bench chair for Regan. He just wished that she'd stop being such a worrywart.

LUKE AND NORA had the news on in their room as they dressed for dinner. But every two minutes Nora pressed the mute button on the remote control and answered the phone. It was obviously the hour when people had gone back to their rooms to get ready for the evening and they had found their invitations to the cocktail party and fashion show waiting for them.

The acceptances were rolling in.

Nora kept a list by the phone and checked off the names as they called.

"Honey," Luke said, "why don't you finish getting dressed? I'm all ready. I'll answer the phone."

"Thanks, dear," Nora said, "but you've been busy all day. Just sit and watch the news."

"I haven't heard one story all the way through anyway,'' he said wryly as the phone rang and Nora pressed the mute button again.

''Well, okay,'' Nora said as she handed him her pen and the remote control and disappeared into the bathroom.

''Hello,'' Luke's deep voice boomed. ''Yes, this is Nora Regan Reilly's room. No, we won't be selling books at the party tomorrow. I believe there are some on sale in the lobby store . . . they're all sold out? I'm sorry. Maybe in town you could pick one up . . . no, I don't know the name of the nearest bookstore . . . your name? Thank you. See you tomorrow.'' He hung up the phone as Nora came out of the bathroom.

''This party is doing wonders for your royalty statements.''

''It's supposed to sell panty hose, not books,'' Nora said as she slipped into her heels.

The phone rang again.

''You can get it if you want,'' Luke sighed. ''There's a commercial on that looks very interesting.''

Nora laughed. ''Hello . . . yes, this is the place to call about the party . . . Ruth Craddock . . . I'm happy you can make it, Ruth . . . yes, lots of people are coming . . . hello? . . . hello?'' Nora hung up the phone. ''She was in an awful hurry to get off the phone.''

''She's got the right idea,'' Luke mumbled. ''Before it rings again, let's get out of here.''

''I just have to check my face,'' Nora said.

''It's still there,'' Luke assured her.

''Oh, I almost forgot! I've got to wear Richie's panty

hose!'' Nora quickly pulled them out of the drawer. ''Do you want to start downstairs?''

''No, I'll wait for you,'' Luke said as he settled back on the bed. ''*Gone With the Wind* is just starting on The Movie Channel, and I've never seen it all the way through.''

RUTH SAT TWITCHING at the desk in the Calla-Lily suite. She was right, as usual. She had just hung up after being told that lots of people were going to the cocktail party tomorrow. Great. Just great.

"Ethel!" she screamed.

Ethel peered around the corner of the kitchenette where she was making a cup of tea for herself. Today had been such a bad day that she'd only had time for a couple of cups. She hadn't dared ask for her afternoon break. That was always when she liked to sip her tea, have a brownie, and read the paper. And now they were into the dinner hour and Ethel knew better than to ask if she could go home. "Yes, Ruth," she said.

"Ethel, I'm out of cigarettes!"

"Right here, Ruth." Ethel pulled open the refrigerator, which she had stocked with cartons of Ruth's brand. If there was anything worse than Ruth in a bad mood, it was Ruth in a bad mood and going through nicotine withdrawal. If I don't have a heart attack working for her, Ethel thought as she opened the carton and retrieved a pack, her secondhand smoke will definitely kill me.

Ethel threw the cellophane in the garbage. It's not hard to figure out why they pay me so well, she thought. But if I won the lottery this minute, I'd be out of here so fast her head would spin, and Ruthless would be on her hands and knees picking up these cigarettes off the floor. And then, Ethel thought, I'd have lots of free time to spend with my grandchildren.

With a longing look at her cup of tea, she went into the living room. "Here you go, Ruth," Ethel said, trying to sound gracious.

"Thank you, Ethel," Ruth rasped. As she lit her cigarette, Ruth's mouth movements reminded Ethel of a baby getting a good hold on its pacifier after it had been lost.

"From now on, Ethel," Ruth pronounced as she exhaled, "whenever anyone from Calla-Lily goes on vacation, they have to wear a beeper."

"Umm-hmmmm. Good idea, Ruth," Ethel said.

"That way we'll never run into this trouble again. If, of course, we're still in business!" Ruth started to shake. "I would just be so happy if Irving found something wrong with those panty hose. It'd be such a relief, I'd feel like a new person."

I doubt I'd mistake you for Mother Teresa, Ethel thought.

"Now," Ruth said, "all the board members know that they're to meet here early tomorrow morning, do they not?"

Ethel nodded vehemently. "Everyone knows, except, of course," she hesitated, "the one we haven't been able to locate."

A low growl emanated from Ruth's throat. "Jungle Jim. They're still working on finding him, aren't they?"

"Yes. They're going to call as soon as there's any news."

"We have the cashier's check ready just in case?"

"It's all taken care of. Five million dollars."

Ruth grimaced. "And the papers have been drawn up so we can make a deal with this Blossom guy?"

"They're all ready to be signed. If the board agrees to it, you're all set to hand over the five million dollars and—"

"ALL RIGHT, Ethel." Ruth paused to collect herself. "Irving is in the lab, where I trust he will remain for the rest of the night, testing and retesting these indestructible panty hose, these pieces of fabric that could ruin my life. If he finds a way to snag them, my prayers will be answered."

Who do you pray to? Ethel wondered.

"And if he doesn't, we have to be the ones to take control of them. I've got to get downstairs to the rubber-chicken dinner. Just what I really feel like having. A lot of small talk when I have other things to think about. I trust you will remain here awaiting word as to the whereabouts of our overgrown Boy Scout."

Ethel managed a smile. "I'll be here."

"Good. I know it's late. You can turn on the television if you'd like."

"Thank you, Ruth."

"No problem, Ethel." Ruth started to leave when Ethel suddenly remembered.

"Oh, Ruth. One more thing. While you were on the other line, Barney Freize called. He's looking for his money."

Ruth swung around, her eyes bulging. "You call Barney and tell him we'll have his commission check of forty-five thousand dollars as soon as we know if the panty hose is good. He's already gotten five thousand dollars for letting us have first crack at it."

"But—" Ethel protested.

"No buts! Just do it!" Ruth slammed the door behind her.

In my own sweet time, Ethel thought indignantly as she picked up the hotel television guide.

A T FIVE MINUTES past seven, Regan and Richie's taxi pulled up in front of the Watergreen Hotel. A doorman rushed over to let them out.

"Welcome to the Watergreen."

"Thank you," Regan said as she got out behind Richie. Two well-dressed couples were waiting to hop in.

"Where are you going to?" the doorman asked them.

"Joe's Stone Crab," one of the women said excitedly.

"I hope you've got a reservation," he replied and leaned over to tell the cabbie.

"Last I heard, they don't take reservations," Regan heard one of the men mumble.

Regan pushed through the revolving doors of the hotel, with Richie following. They stepped into a dazzling lobby with bright green-and-white-checked carpeting, numerous plants, and a miniature waterfall on a side wall. The registration desk was to the left. Across the way was a sunken area with a large circular bar, and tables and chairs that had a great view of the pools outside and the beach that lay beyond. The whole effect was festive.

Regan spotted Maura and John seated by themselves. She and Richie hurried over.

"How's the blushing bride?" Regan asked as they all kissed hello.

"On my third nervous breakdown," Maura replied.

"Fourth," John corrected. "Here, have a seat. No one else has shown up yet."

Regan and Richie sat down and the waiter hurried over. Richie ordered an old-fashioned and Regan decided to have a mai-tai.

"Yours looks so good," she said to Maura.

"It's so good I'm already on my second."

"Your hair looks nice," Regan said.

"You think so? It's a wig."

"It is not," Regan said flatly with a half-smile.

"I know. But I'm beginning to think that's the way to go."

"Don't laugh," Richie said. "Poor Birdie tried one of those home permanents a few days before we got married. It looked like someone came up behind her and scared her real bad. She couldn't stop crying. God love her. I told her not to worry, it'd all be okay. But I must say I was relieved when it grew out about a year later."

"Uncle Richie, did she wear a wig at your wedding?" Maura asked.

"She wanted to, but her mother thought it was sacrilegious. I know. Go figure." Richie helped himself to peanuts.

"So, John," Regan said, "do you have any cute single friends who are going to be at the wedding?"

John's face, handsome with its sparkling Irish eyes and strong features framed by curly blond hair, settled into a frown. "Now, let me think . . ."

"That means no," Maura pronounced.

"What about Kyle?" John protested.

"Kyle?" Maura gasped. "I'm not setting up one of my oldest and best friends with Kyle. He's a pathological liar."

John nodded his head. "That's true. But other than that, he's a really nice guy."

Maura turned to Regan. "We used to double-date with him until I couldn't take it anymore. One night we'd be with one girl who'd be telling me all about her and Kyle's plans for the future. The next night there'd be someone else he was leading on. I couldn't stand it because I wanted to tell them, but John would have killed me."

"Gee, I can't wait to meet him," Regan retorted. "Oh, look, here come my parents."

Nora and Luke hurried over from the elevator bank and greeted everyone.

"Good news, Richie," Nora said as they sat down. "We're getting lots of responses for the party."

"Oh, that's great, Nora. A lot of people, huh?"

"Believe me, a lot of people," Luke testified.

Nora patted Maura's hand. "And the big day is almost here."

"That it is. You're coming to the luncheon tomorrow, aren't you?"

"Absolutely. The fashion show isn't until three o'clock. What time does the rehearsal dinner start?"

"Drinks at seven."

Regan laughed. "I've got some good stories for the toasts."

"That's what I'm afraid of," Maura groaned.

"Spring break in college. I came down to visit you. What was that guy's name again? The one who gave you his college ring five minutes after you met him at that bar in Fort Lauderdale?"

"REGAN!"

"Their whole relationship lasted about an hour and a half. Irreconcilable differences."

"I didn't hear about this one," John observed.

"That's because no one counted until I met you," Maura said, her voice dripping with sweetness.

"Thank God you broke off the engagement to that other guy a few years ago," Richie pronounced as he munched on more peanuts. "He was all wrong for you."

"I knew we should have eloped. Let's change the subject," Maura pleaded.

John put his arm around her. "We have no secrets, honey." He turned to Regan. "What else can you tell me?"

"Did she ever mention the guy who gave her a set of

jumper cables for Christmas? The worst part was that they weren't even wrapped.''

"He also gave her a set of windshield wipers," Richie offered.

"Oh yes," Regan chuckled, "he was a hopeless romantic.''

Maura hit John's knee. "I can't wait to get a couple of your friends contributing to the storytelling.''

"Now, now," Nora said. "Let's not pick on Maura.''

"We'll have plenty of time for that tomorrow night," Regan agreed.

The waiter came by and Luke and Nora ordered their drinks.

"Maura, what kind of music are you going to have at the reception?" Nora asked.

"Elevator music, if my mother has her way.''

"At least nobody will start to sweat when they dance," Regan offered.

"Actually," Maura began, "we've hired a band that plays all kinds of music. Or so they say. My mother's afraid that when they start playing rock and roll they'll blast the place out, so she's begging them to leave their amplifiers at home.''

"Speaking of amplifiers," Regan said, "we need to figure out what we're going to use for a sound system for the fashion show.''

"We just got a set of pots and pans you can borrow," Maura offered.

"We'll have to save those for New Year's Eve," Regan said.

The waiter appeared and deposited Luke's and Nora's drinks on the table. "Excuse me," Nora said, "do you know if the manager, Mr. Fargus, is still here?"

"I'll check for you, ma'am."

"Nick Fargus?" Maura said. "He helped us plan the reception. He's definitely a little weird."

Luke chuckled.

Nora looked at him.

"I know, Dad," Regan said. "Mom was looking to fix me up with him, right?"

"I didn't say a word," Luke said as he put up his hands.

"He is a lovely young man," Nora insisted.

Within minutes, Nick was scurrying over to the table, checking for dust buildup on the brass railings along his way.

"Hello, hello, hello, everyone. Hello, Maura. Hello, John. Hello, Mrs. Reilly. Hello, Mr. Reilly."

"Hello, Nick," Nora said. "I'd like you to meet my daughter, Regan—"

"Oh, nice to meet you, Regan. I thought you were one of the models for the fashion show tomorrow."

"No, no. I'm just helping Richie get the show organized. This is Richie Blossom."

"Regan is one of my bridesmaids," Maura said gleefully as Nick and Richie shook hands. "And we were just saying that there aren't enough eligible guys to dance with at the wedding. I do hope you'll stop by and take Regan for a spin on the floor."

"Hey, that's my job! Make everybody happy."

"Thank you," Regan said. "Yes, thank you very

much." I'll get you for this, Maura, she thought. "Do you have a stereo system?"

"A what?"

"A stereo system. We need music for the fashion show."

Nick snapped his fingers. "You know something? I don't. I've been meaning to buy a CD player, but I've been so darn busy. I knew I should have just gone out and gotten one. I wanted to read *Consumers Digest* to find out which was the best one to get, and now it's tomorrow—" His voice trailed off mournfully.

"Don't worry," Regan said as she unconsciously patted his shoulder.

"You still want to have the fashion show, don't you?" Nick asked.

"Of course," Regan said. "If I can get ahold of a friend of mine who is a stereo salesman and knows all about which one to buy, would you be interested in making a quick purchase tomorrow morning?"

Nick nodded. "You bet."

"Good." Now, I hope I have Nadine's number with me, Regan thought.

NADINE AND JOEY were enjoying a cold beer on the patio in his backyard when the phone rang.

"Why don't you let the machine pick it up?" Nadine asked as she curled her toes around the braiding of the chaise longue.

"It might be the office." Joey hurried into the kitchen.

A minute later he was yelling out the kitchen window, "Nay, it's for you."

"For me?"

"It's Regan."

"Regan?"

"Do I hear an echo?" Joey asked.

"Wiseass," Nadine said as she pulled herself out of the chair. "I don't know why they don't get a cordless phone for this house,'' she mumbled, ''a little static in your ear never hurt anybody.''

The screen door slammed behind her as she took the phone from Joey. ''Hey, Regan, what's up?''

Nadine listened as Regan explained to her about the fashion show and the urgent need for a compact disc player.

''You're not going to believe this, Regan, but today I met a woman who claims she was wearing this run-proof panty hose. It was really nice.''

''Where did she get it?'' Regan asked.

''Her son is an engineer and he's testing it for his company to possibly buy. Oh, hi.''

''What?'' Regan said.

''Sorry, one of Joey's roommates just walked in. Anyway, we were both getting a manicure and I knocked into this woman's leg with my wet nails. The polish wiped right off. Your friend Richie could make a lot of money on those stockings if they're as good as they seem. I'd buy ten pairs.''

''That's what we're hoping,'' Regan said, ''which of course comes back to the need for the compact disc player. Can you recommend a particular kind? This guy Nick wants to run out and buy one tomorrow morning.''

''It depends on how much he wants to spend,'' Nadine said. ''Some people drive me crazy coming in and out of the store a hundred times, checking every last detail of every system, down to the color of the plug. I know they're really running around wasting gas comparing prices all over town. What's this guy like, anyway?''

''Ohhhhh, he's nice,'' Regan said haltingly.

"Nice means uh-oh," Nadine said as she sat down on one of the vinyl kitchen chairs whose stuffing was popping out in the back. "Before I met Joey, when someone tried to fix me up, if they started out by saying 'Well, he's nice,' you knew that was the kiss of death."

Regan laughed. "My mother thinks he's a lovely young man."

"Enough said. Wait a minute, how did your mother meet him?"

"She and my father are down here for a convention and for the wedding. She's hosting the cocktail party before the fashion show."

"Cool. Regan, I can tell you a lot of things to look for in a CD system, but it's probably better if I go shopping with him. Hold on. Joey, are you going to work in the morning?"

"For a couple of hours."

"Regan, if he wants, I can go with him in the morning."

"Nadine, that would be really nice of you. Are you sure?"

"Yeah. Besides, Joey and I can go to the beach tomorrow afternoon."

"You're certainly welcome to come to the cocktail party and fashion show."

"That might be fun. Old Nick'll probably need help setting up the CD player in his apartment anyway."

"I'm sure. I'd come shopping with you, but the bridesmaids are getting together at eleven A.M. for a luncheon. But I can meet you here at the hotel afterward."

"That's fine. Why don't you come over for a beer later? We're just going to cook some food and hang out with some of Joey's friends and his roommates."

"I probably won't get finished here until ten," Regan said. "Is that too late?"

"Are you kidding? In this part of town, the night hasn't even started yet."

"True. Give me your address."

After Nadine gave Regan the address, they agreed that Regan would have Nick call Nadine directly to set up their shopping date for the next morning.

"He's with our group right now," Regan said, "we're about to go in for dinner. I'll have him call you right away."

"I'll be here. By the way, Regan, do you have a boyfriend?"

"Why are you asking me that, Nadine?"

"Because I've got a guy here who you should meet."

"Only if he's really nice. Bye, Nadine."

"Bye, Regan."

BARNEY FREIZE WAS more than a little annoyed that Ruth Craddock didn't have the decency to call him back after he had been good enough to introduce her to the Birdie Panty Hose and very possibly save her company's butt. Barney paced around his little den. "It takes nerve, that's what it takes, it takes nerve," he said to the air. He pulled open the sliding glass doors that opened onto his tiny backyard and breathed in the pungent scent of the citrus trees. "Be calm, Barn, be calm," he said to himself but felt his anger rising.

Here he was hanging, waiting for a callback from the queen of the cotton crotch. Three times today the secretary had told him, "Sorry, sir, but she's in a meeting." Yeah, and I'm the Tooth Fairy, he thought.

I didn't have to go to Calla-Lily with the Birdie Panty Hose. I could just as easily have hopped a plane to North Carolina, where so many of the other panty-hose companies are located, and let one of them in on the big secret. He'd worked back there years ago and could have gotten in to see the big shots. If they had seen it, felt it, worn it, they would have known it was good. You can't believe what you read in a letter, especially from some dodo like Richie.

The other day over at Calla-Lily Ruth had told him that the tests were all positive, but they still weren't sure. For God's sake, the panty-hose convention is going on right now. Was she going to try and stiff him out of his big fee? She'd better not.

Barney walked into the kitchen and pulled open the refrigerator. This is all thanks to my nephew Danny, he thought. Danny had volunteered to get him in to see Ruth when Barney had told him, in deepest confidence, about the panty hose. It had all been so easy, it was almost surprising.

But Danny was doing the yard work for her at Casa Panty Hose. He dealt directly with Ruth. She was just getting rid of another husband. Maybe Danny had talked to her today and knew what was going on.

I'll call him, Barney thought. He shut the refrigerator door, picked up the phone and dialed his nephew's number. Danny's machine picked up. "Hi, this is Danny. I'm not home right now but if you leave your name and number . . ." It figures, Barney thought. What twenty-five-year-old kid is going to be home on a Friday night? Especially a good-looking kid like Danny.

"Danny, this is Uncle Barney. Give me a call, would you? It's important."

Barney hung up the phone. I'll probably hear back from him in another three days, he thought.

Now what am I going to do about dinner? I'll light a cigar first, that's what I'll do.

Barney went back to his cozy little den and sat down in his favorite place, a recliner chair that went back just far enough so that he could comfortably doze off watching television without waking up with a stiff neck. He opened the cigar box he had situated within arm's reach of this perch and pulled out a brand-new White Owl, sniffing it appreciatively. This would relax him. Alone and free with his cigar, and no one around to chase him outside to smoke it, like his ex-wife used to do. Of course she never minded the smell of cigar smoke when they were dating, but once they got married, boom, that was it. No cigar smoking in the house. He'd had about all he was going to take of that. This little room stank of cigar smoke, and he loved every whiff.

Barney held the lighter he had found on the beach under his cigar and watched it flicker as he inhaled. The whole ritual had a religious feel to it. When the cigar was finally lit, he pushed back in his seat, stretching out his legs on the footrest attached to his La-Z-Boy, which obediently appeared and disappeared at Barney's will. Whoever said a man's home was his castle was no idiot, Barney thought.

As he puffed, he listened to the sounds of the night in his backyard. The insects, an occasional plane flying by, the rustle of the breeze.

I could use the money, he thought. Another $45,000 if those panty hose are the real thing. And it looks like they are.

I'll enjoy my cigar for a little while, I'll make myself some dinner, and I'll wait for my callback. If I don't get it, he thought, I'll just have to figure out how to handle that Ruth Craddock.

J UDD GREEN SAT at a table in one of the dining rooms of the Watergreen Hotel. The group he'd been watching had just settled at a large table nearby. He'd made sure his table was close enough to theirs for good viewing and eavesdropping.

Regan Reilly, the girl who was Richie Blossom's shadow, was making an announcement. He strained to listen.

"Good news, Richie," Regan said as the waiter ceremoniously fluffed her napkin and placed it on her lap. She nodded her thanks as she continued. "I just talked to my friend Nadine. She bumped into someone today at a nail salon who was wearing what sounds like your Birdie Panty Hose. She says they're great. Her son-in-law is an engineer for a panty hose company that might be interested in buying them. He's in charge of testing them.''

"All right, Richie," Ed Durkin cheered. "We'll have a double celebration this weekend."

Richie jumped up. "What company does this guy work for? How did he get my panty hose?''

"Richie, you have given a lot of pairs away," Regan said.

"But just to my friends," Richie told her.

"You do have patent protection, don't you?" Regan asked, alarmed.

"Oh, sure.''

"Then you don't have to worry. I'm going to see Nadine later. I'll find out what she knows, if anything, about the company testing it.''

"Oh, God, I don't believe it!" Richie said exuberantly. He held up his water glass. "I propose a toast to Birdie's legs and Birdie's legacy.''

Regan felt a sudden worry. "Richie," she warned, "we better not count our chickens before they're hatched. This is a good sign, but until you've received and accepted an offer, anything can go wrong.''

"Regan, you're a worrywart. If this company doesn't come through, another one will." Richie's smile faded. A concerned frown creased his forehead. "Of course if they don't come through this weekend, it'll be too late for the Fourth Quarter.''

"Don't think about that, Richie," Nora said soothingly. "We're going to give the best cocktail party this place has ever seen. We'll end up with a bidding war." She held out her leg and gave it a quick swing. "I love your panty hose."

Maura's mother, Bridget, agreed. "I love them too. I'm wearing them now. And Richie gave me a pair that perfectly matches my mother-of-the bride dress."

"Is that the same dress you were going to wear to Maura's wedding two years ago?" Regan asked sweetly.

"No. She put it in long-term storage for your mother, Regan," Maura said.

"Touché," Regan grinned.

"Seriously, Richie," Nora said, "they are lovely. If I owned a hosiery company, I wouldn't want to be competing in the marketplace with the Birdie Panty Hose. These are so good they could easily put everyone else out of business. If some company is testing them and realizes how good they are, and knows you're going to be showing them off tomorrow, you might get an offer before the fashion show."

"Provided it's Richie's panty hose they're testing," Luke warned.

"Of course," Nora agreed.

"At least we don't have to worry about *our* business, right, Luke?" Ed asked. "The only things you can be sure of in this world are—"

"Death and taxes," the whole group said aloud, having heard this proverb from Ed at least a hundred times before.

Maura and Regan exchanged looks before Maura turned to John. "Now you know why my brother's an accountant."

They ordered drinks and while they were sipping, the captain appeared to announce the specials.

"My favorite for tonight," he began as he kissed his fingers, "is"—he kissed them again—"frogs' legs!"

"That's a sign from Birdie," Richie announced, beaming.

A few tables away the solitary diner, Judd Green, ordered his dinner mechanically. From the sounds of it, things were coming to a head sooner than they had expected. There wasn't much time left.

When the conversation at the large table turned to talk about a wedding, he no longer paid close attention.

Regan Reilly was going to visit a friend tonight. It sounded as though she or someone else would drop Richie Blossom off at the Fourth Quarter. He'd tipped the valet to leave his car right out on the street in front of the hotel. He had to be ready to move as soon as he saw which car Richie Blossom got into.

Hurriedly he picked at his dinner and ordered coffee. It might be a long night.

When the coffee came, he asked for his check.

"Certainly," the waiter said cheerfully as he poured the steaming brew into his cup and was bumped from behind by a busboy. A few drops of coffee spattered onto Green's scraped hand. He yanked his hand back, cursing.

"I'm so sorry, Mr. Evans," the waiter stammered.

With difficulty Green calmed himself. The waiter had raised his voice and he sensed other diners were glancing at them. He did not want to attract attention.

"That hand looks nasty," the waiter continued. "That's some scrape you've got there."

"It's all right," he said testily. "Just get me my check, please."

"How about a drink on the house?" The waiter was determined to make amends.

For the third time Judd Green, aka Lowell Evans, requested his check.

"Right away, right away." The waiter hurried off.

When Judd Green finally signed his check, he noticed that Richie Blossom and his group were ordering dessert. He was outside waiting in his car when they emerged half an hour later.

A MILD BURP escaped from Ethel's lips as she folded up her napkin. That was mighty good, she thought. Nibbling on a bread crumb that had escaped previous detection, she surveyed the table that room service had wheeled in with her dinner. A single rose in a crystal vase was surrounded by the remains of shrimp cocktail, steak au poivre, pommes frites, and zucchini squash. Her salad plate contained microscopic traces of arugula and endive. A half bottle of wine had been emptied and the tricolor sherbet was a memory. Ethel made one final attempt to shake more liquid from the coffee pot and was rewarded with a few precious drops.

Maybe Ruth is eating rubber chicken, she gloated, but not me. If I have to stay and mind the store, then

the store has to buy me dinner. Ruth knew I had to eat
but, sorry, boss, McDonald's doesn't deliver.

Ethel stood up. No use flaunting it. I better get this
table out of here before Ruth figures out what I ordered.
And I'll open the window so she doesn't smell the steak.

Ethel glanced at her watch. They should be on the
banquet speeches by now, she thought happily, knowing
how much Ruth hated them. Ethel hoped the president
of the National Panty-Hose Association dragged out that
same old speech about the history of limb coverings.
That was a real snore. She giggled to herself. Is it
because I'm getting older that I'm having these nasty
thoughts and feel free to enjoy them? Is it that all these
torturous years of working for Ruth have finally hit me?
Or, Ethel thought naughtily, could it be this delicious
bottle of expensive wine?

As she opened the window, the phone began to ring.
"Cominggg," she sang.

"Hello. Calla-Lily."

A male voice spoke from what sounded like a black
hole. "This is the search party for Preston Landers. Is
Ruth Craddock there?"

"No, this is Ethel."

"Oh, hi, Ethel."

"Well, how's it going?" she asked.

"We've got good news and bad news."

Ethel sat on the couch, wishing it had all been bad
news. "Well, what's the bad news?"

"Most people want to hear the good news first."

"Suit yourself."

"Okay. The good news is that we're closing in on him. He's still in Colorado somewhere. His team picked up supplies at the outpost we're at now just a few hours ago. The bad news is we've got to call off the search until the crack of dawn."

"It all sounds so exciting," Ethel remarked.

"You betcha. Pass the word along that we intend to get him back there in time for Ms. Craddock's important meeting."

"The meeting starts at seven A.M. tomorrow morning."

"I didn't say he'd be on time. But we'll get him there."

"I'll let her know. Good luck." He should be wishing me good luck, Ethel thought.

"You betcha. Have a good night now." The line was disconnected.

"Over and out," Ethel said as she hung up the phone. After a moment she picked it up again and dialed room service. "Could you please come and collect my dinner cart as soon as possible? . . . Yes, everything was more than satisfactory. I can't wait to order breakfast . . . no, I'm just kidding, I'm not staying here . . . thank you."

Ethel suddenly jumped up. I never called that Freize guy. She hurried over to the desk where she had jotted down his number. Quickly she dialed. He answered almost immediately.

"Mr. Freize, this is Ruth Craddock's secretary, Ethel . . . Yes, I know it's taken a while to get back to you, but Ms. Craddock asked me to call you and tell you that you can come by tomorrow morning. That's when we'll finally know if the panty hose will be purchased. If so, we'll give you the check.''

At the other end of the phone, Barney sighed. ''To tell you the truth, I didn't think she was going to pay me.''

''Ohhh,'' Ethel clucked, ''she's been rather preoccupied.''

The doorbell to the suite rang. ''Hold on, Mr. Freize.''

Ethel opened the door to the smiling room-service attendant, who hurried in and efficiently disassembled the sides of the table. ''Looks as if you enjoyed your meal, ma'am.''

''No use feeding the garbage can,'' Ethel replied.

''That's certainly right. Now, if you'd like anything else, just give us a call. We're open twenty-four hours.''

''I need my job.''

''Excuse me?''

''Never mind. Good night.''

''Good night, now.'' He opened the door and Ethel watched the last vestiges of her dinner disappear around the corner.

''Mr. Freize . . .''

''I'm here.''

The phone in the bedroom where Ruth was staying began to ring. Oh, dear, Ethel thought. That might be the search party calling back on the other line because this one is busy. ''Mr. Freize, could you please hold on?''

''Why not?''

"Thank you." Ethel hurried into Ruth's bedroom, where the phone was insistently ringing. She dived for it before voice mail picked it up. "Hello," she gasped.

"Ruthy Wuthy," a young male voice cooed, "you sound sooo tiiii-ruddd."

Ethel sat up on the bed. "This isn't Ruthy—ahh—I mean Ruth. This is Ethel. Who may I ask is calling?"

The caller hung up so fast, Ethel blinked. Well, Ethel thought wickedly, what shall I tell Ruthy Wuthy when she asks if there were any calls? She shrugged and hurried back to Barney.

"Mr. Freize?"

"I'm here."

"I'm so sorry. Things are so hectic around here."

Barney hesitated and then decided to go for it. She had kept him waiting several times now. "Ethel," he began, "do you get any intimation as to whether the sale of the panty-hose patent to Calla-Lily will go through? I mean, you're right there in the thick of things."

You're not kidding, Ethel thought, but she straightened up and said, "I'm sorry, Mr. Freize, but I am not at liberty to discuss the matter. I was just told to tell you that we'll know tomorrow."

"You'll be seeing me then."

For the third time in ten minutes, Ethel wasn't given the chance to bid adieu to her gentlemen callers.

IRVING FRANKLIN SAT at the head of his dining-room table sipping his after-dinner tea as he listened to his mother-in-law's incessant chatter.

"Fern," she was saying as she held out her manicured hands to her daughter, "do you like this color? I don't know . . . I think there might be too much brown in it. When I had my colors done last year, they said I should stay away from brown."

"They look nice, Mother," Fern said wearily.

"Yeah, well, I'm not sure. Tammy's not here, so I can't ask her. What do you think, Irving?"

Irving put down his teacup. Deep down he wanted to say that he couldn't care less, but he caught the pleading look in his wife's eyes. "I think it's a very flattering shade, Mom."

He hated to call her Mom. It made him feel disloyal to his own dear departed mother, but it had started years ago when Fern's sister's husband decided to call her Mom. Easy for him. He didn't have to live with her. But most of the time Irving avoided the problem by not addressing her at all. He threw it in now to please Fern, who smiled back at him gratefully.

"Maybe next week I'll try a different shade. I don't know. Are you two going to a movie tonight?"

"Irving still has work to do," Fern answered softly.

"More work? You're always poking around downstairs in that lab of yours. It's Friday night."

"The panty-hose tests must be completed by tomorrow morning," Irving said with a steely grin.

"I was telling the girls at the nail salon about them today. I said how wonderful they are."

"We're not supposed to talk about them, remember?" Irving asked, his voice going up ever so slightly.

"Mom" looked at him sourly. "Well, I can tell you another test they passed, if it'll make you happy. The girl next to me smeared her polish on them accidentally and it wiped right off."

"It did?"

"That's right," she said smugly. "I bet you never thought of that test in that dungeon of yours."

Irving pushed back his chair. "All my *laboratory* tests are not complete. I'm still trying to break down the ingredients of the fabric. I personally believe there's got to be something wrong with those panty hose and," he paused, "I intend to find out just what it is." He kissed his wife on the top of her head. ''Fern darling, let me know if you need me.''

As he closed the basement door behind him he happily shut out the sound of ''There was another color that had a little more red in it that I think would have been better, but . . .''

THAT WAS REALLY fun, wasn't it, hon?'' Nora asked as she and Luke stepped off the elevator.

"We always have a good time with the Durkins, don't we?'' Luke agreed. "I'm looking forward to the wedding on Sunday. By then we'll be through with the fashion show and all my meetings . . . we can really let loose.'' He put his arm around Nora, grabbed her hand, and danced with her down the hallway.

"One-two-three, one-two-three, one-two-three,'' Luke sang.

"Oh, my,'' Nora laughed as they reached the door. "When Regan gets married, we'll have to—''

"Nora!'' Luke admonished.

"I'm sorry. I couldn't help it but I was just thinking . . .''

Luke opened the door. "One wedding at a time. This one is Maura's." He pointed to the room. "After you, my dear."

Nora sighed. "Okay. Let's see if we got any more messages about the fashion show."

"I can't wait," Luke drawled.

Nora went over and picked up the phone. An electronic voice told her that they had received ten messages. She sat down and started to write them down as they played back. The first nine were from people RSVP-ing to the cocktail party. They'd all be happy to come. The tenth message started to play in Nora's ear.

A well-modulated voice said, "Hello, Mrs. Reilly; my name is Dayton Rotter. I met some of the models who will be in your fashion show tomorrow. Technically I'm down here from New York City for a few days' vacation, but I'm a venture capitalist and we're never really off." He laughed. "This panty hose sounds intriguing, and I was wondering if I could come by your cocktail party tomorrow." Nora scribbled down his number.

"Luke, you're not going to believe this!" she exclaimed.

"What?" Luke asked as he hung up his jacket and loosened his tie.

"Dayton Rotter wants to come to the cocktail party!"

"*The* Dayton Rotter?"

"It sounds like him. It must be him. He met some of the models and wants to check out the panty hose."

Luke whistled. "He's big. That could be just what Richie needs. Did he leave a number?"

"Yes."

"Well, call him back."

"I am, I am."

Nora dialed the number and sat tapping the desk with her pen. When a man's voice answered the phone, it sounded as though he was in a crowded bar.

"This is Nora Regan Reilly. Is Dayton Rotter there?"

"It's me," he said. "Sorry about the noise. I'm at a club right now. I've got my cellular phone with me."

Surprise, surprise, Nora thought.

"I got your message," she said, "and we'd be delighted if you came to the party tomorrow. We really think that this panty hose is something special."

Luke smiled at her and raised his eyebrows.

Nora strained to hear Dayton's voice and separate it from the blare of the music in the background.

"That's great," Dayton almost yelled. "I'd very much like to be there. Quite frankly, if the product is as good as the young ladies say it is, I'd be very interested in developing it. After all, my business is to find good ideas and run with them. By the way, I like your books."

Nora smiled broadly. "Oh, thank you. We'll see you tomorrow then."

"He likes your books?" Luke asked when Nora hung up.

"You do know me, don't you?"

"After thirty-five years, I would hope so. We'll have to spread the word that he's coming. The sight of that guy will get people bidding." Luke sat on the bed and untied his shoes.

"I'll call Nick in the morning. And Richie and Regan. Oh, Luke, I really hope this works out. It would make for such a perfect weekend."

Luke got up and walked toward the bathroom. "That and if Regan catches the bouquet on Sunday," he said as he closed the door just in time to avoid being hit by his wife's airborne terry-cloth slipper.

LUCILLE LEANED BACK on the pillows of her sister Dolly's bed as she talked on the rotary phone to her friend Arthur. She had just come upstairs after having a potluck dinner in the Dolly Twiggs Memorial Room.

"The service was so, so lovely, Arthur. I wish you could have been there. Everyone here just loved Dolly. We all broke bread together afterward." She paused. "What did you have for dinner, dear?"

A second later Lucille bolted upright on the bed. "What do you mean, Mildred brought over a tuna casserole? I left you plenty of frozen food you could have heated in the microwave . . . She says fresh food is better, does she? . . ."

Lucille felt herself begin to hyperventilate as she listened to Arthur tell her how delicious Mildred's casserole really was; not too fishy, just right. But when he started to suggest that she should give the folks at the Fourth Quarter an extension, she really began to have an out-of-body experience.

She swallowed hard. "Arthur, I can't afford to give them an extension. I get so depressed when I'm here." Tears filled her eyes. "I just want to get back home."

As she listened, the tears spilled down her cheeks. "Oh, I love you too, sweetness. I know you were just trying to be helpful. I miss you too." She covered the mouthpiece and sniffled. "I'll be home in time for your birthday next week. I already know what kind of cake I'm going to make you . . . Mildred's offered to have a party for you?! You didn't say yes, did you? . . . You told her you'd check with me? Tell her the answer is no, you've already got plans."

Five minutes later, when she hung up the phone, Lucille stuck out her jaw. Business is business, she thought. If I don't get home soon, Arthur will slip through my fingers. In their retirement village there must be ten women for every man, and he was the most handsome man left, not to mention the healthiest.

Lucille stood up. I need some air, she thought. After that conversation, I certainly don't feel sleepy. I'll go downstairs and watch the weirdos wander by.

Outside, Lucille flipped open a beach chair and sat down. No one else from the Fourth Quarter was around. But it was a Friday night and the street was buzzing.

Singles, couples, groups passed by. One outfit is

skimpier than the next, Lucille thought. Don't they ever catch a cold?

A taxi pulled up and stopped. The door opened. Richie got out and Lucille heard him say, "Yes, I'm going to stay home. I'll talk to you in the morning." He turned around and waved to Lucille as he walked up the sidewalk.

"You're out here by yourself? Where is everybody?"

"I think there's a program they wanted to watch tonight."

"Mind if I join you?" Richie asked.

"Of course not. This is your place."

"Let's hope so," Richie joked, but the remark hung in the air. "Are you okay, Lucille?"

Her lip quivered. "I suppose. Being here is hard for me. I miss Dolly so much. And now I have this boyfriend Arthur, and I'm missing him too."

Richie sat down.

"Someone made him a casserole tonight," Lucille sputtered.

"Oh, God," Richie said. "Oh, God."

"Mildred is a pest and I know it shouldn't get me upset because Arthur's not interested in her." Lucille wiped her eyes. "But I'm still scared. I'm hurting from losing Dolly a year ago, and now Arthur has just started to fill that void in my heart that I've had since my husband died."

"You were married before?" Richie asked gently.

"For forty-five wonderful years."

"Birdie and I were married forty-eight years. A lot of people would say that makes us pretty lucky."

"I know that. But statistics don't help when you get lonesome."

Richie paused. "You're right. Sometimes I get tired of people telling me how lucky I was to have been happy for so long. I say, what about now?" His voice grew tight. "I wish Birdie were here right this minute; that's what counts."

"Don't I know it," Lucille declared.

"Lucille . . ."

"Yes, Richie."

"Wasn't it hard to start dating after your husband died?"

"Are you kidding me? Of course it was. I never thought I'd look at another man. But one day it just happens. You realize that your spouse would want you to be happy. And then I was lucky enough to meet Arthur."

They sat in silence for a few minutes. Finally Lucille stood up. "I'm going to try and get some rest. Tomorrow is a big day, Richie; you should get some sleep too."

"I'll just sit out here for a few more minutes."

As Lucille walked slowly inside, Richie realized that if tomorrow didn't work out, they could never ask her for an extension. She's got her own life to worry about, he thought.

The screen door swung open and Elmer Pickett stepped outside.

"Hi, Elmer," Richie said.

Elmer stood there staring down at Richie. "You know, Richie, everyone could have used the bonus money the real estate agency was willing to pay us if we gave up the option early. Of course now that you're making the commercials, you don't have to worry."

"I made one commercial, Elmer."

"Whatever. I think you're leading the people in this home down the garden path with this crazy scheme of yours. Some of them are going to end up in the street, when they could have at least left here with a few dollars."

Richie stood up and stared into Elmer's eyes. Through clenched teeth he raised his voice. "It's not a crazy scheme! And we took a vote!"

His heart beating wildly, Richie hurried down the sidewalk and hailed a taxi. I've got to get out to the panty-hose factory, he thought. I want to be around the machines and make sure I have the names of everyone in the business I wrote to. There might even be more panty hose there. Just stepping inside the cab and giving the address made him feel better.

He didn't notice that a car nearby had just pulled out of its parking space and was following him.

REGAN RANG THE bell of Joey's house. As she stood there on the porch she rubbed her neck and rolled her head from side to side. Someone had told her the exercise releases tension. She had never figured out whether that was really true, but it was a good way to pass the time.

The door was pulled open.

"Hi!"

The guy who worked at Richie's modeling agency was standing in front of her.

"Hi!" Regan said back as he let her in. "What are you doing here?"

"I live here."

"You live here?"

206 CAROL HIGGINS CLARK

"Do I hear an echo?" Joey yelled from the living room.

"I'm dating a comedian," Nadine pronounced as she got up to greet Regan. "You know Scott?"

"We met today at the agency." Regan glanced at him. He seemed so much more alive than when she had met him in the office. He certainly was handsome with his wavy dark hair, warm brown eyes, and ingratiating smile.

"Yes," Scott agreed and put his arm around Regan. He explained to Nadine, "She's using some of our models tomorrow in her panty-hose fashion show."

"Small world," Nadine said as she led Regan inside. "Walking through here can be hazardous to your health. Please do so at your own risk."

Regan stepped over a set of barbells and was reminded of the fraternities at her college, especially the one they'd dubbed P.U. Sometimes it felt as though that was another lifetime ago. Being here tonight brought it back in a rush. She laughed. The whole scene made her feel ten years younger. After all, people had got along just fine before vacuums were invented.

"Scott, I didn't know you knew Regan," Nadine commented.

"I didn't know that you knew her. Regan happened to come in with one of our clients today—Richie Blossom."

"Well, I'll have you know she's working hard to save your client from losing his home. You know, the Fourth Quarter."

"I know. Richie's a great guy."

"I'm going to help them get a CD player for the fashion show. And I met someone today wearing those panty hose. They're terrific."

Scott crossed his fingers. "We're all hoping it goes well, Regan."

"Thanks."

"And I hope I'm the one who hands him the papers to sign when he buys the Fourth Quarter," Joey said.

"Nadine," Regan asked, "do you know what company that woman's son-in-law works for?"

"No. But I can call her tomorrow if you want."

The phone rang.

"You get it, Scott. It's always for you," Nadine ordered. "Regan, what would you like to drink?"

"What do you have?"

"Beer, wine, soda. We've got a whole refrigerator full of stuff in the garage."

"I'll take a quick look," Regan offered.

"I'll get it," Nadine protested.

"No, no," Regan said. "I'm not sure what I feel like having."

"Okay, right through the door there."

Regan went through the kitchen and down the two steps to the garage door. She opened it and found, if possible, a bigger mess than in the house.

Stepping outside, she nearly tripped over a pile of newspapers. She kicked them out of her way and almost knocked over a can of gas. Oh, great, she thought. I'll just move it into the corner for safety. From the looks of things, no one in this house has an anal personality that will be disturbed by this rearrangement.

From the refrigerator Regan picked out a can of club soda and walked back inside. She sat down in the living room with Nadine, Joey and Scott.

"How many people live here?" Regan asked.

"Four of us and Nadine," Joey answered.

"Since when am I not a person?" Nadine queried.

"Excuse me. Four most of the time. Five every other weekend."

"That's better. The other guys just went out to hit the clubs. And some of Joey's other friends who were supposed to come over got waylaid by some action over at a café."

"There's plenty of action out there," Regan said. She turned to Scott. "So how do you like the modeling business?"

"Huh," Nadine chortled.

Scott laughed.

"He's in hog heaven," Joey said as he twirled a pillow in the air.

"It's pretty good," Scott replied, ignoring the comments. "What kind of work do you do?"

Regan sipped her drink. "I'm a detective."

"Really?"

"Really."

"Does this room have an echo, or what?" Joey asked again.

The phone rang once more. Quickly Scott escaped to answer it.

"He gets more phone calls," Nadine confided. "All

the models are crazy about him. Can you see why, or what?''

Scott poked his head back into the room. ''That was my date. I've got to go meet her. Good luck tomorrow with the fashion show, Regan.''

''Thanks.''

Nadine looked at Joey. ''I wonder who the lucky one is tonight.''

''Who knows.''

After he was safely gone, Nadine volunteered, ''His family used to be really wealthy, but then they lost it.''

''Nadiiiine,'' Joey whined.

''That's what you told me, Joseph.''

''You're not supposed to go telling people that.''

''Regan's not going to say anything.''

''Don't worry, Joey,'' Regan said. ''Does he have any interest in modeling himself? He would probably do well.''

''Nah,'' Joey said. ''He just wants to learn the business end of it.''

Through the garage door Joey's two other roommates appeared, fresh beers in hand.

''Back so soon?'' Nadine asked.

Matt and Dennis were introduced to Regan.

''We couldn't get a parking space, so we figured forget it,'' Dennis explained. ''I'm tired anyway.''

''Well, sit down and talk to us,'' Nadine urged.

Regan drained her can of club soda.

''Would you like something else?'' Nadine asked as Matt and Dennis made themselves comfortable.

''I must be thirsty. But I'll get it.'' Regan went back

out to the garage, careful not to trip over anything this time. She pulled out another can of club soda and noticed that the red gas can was not where she had left it. I don't give these guys enough credit, she thought. One of them must have an anal personality.

RICHIE LET HIMSELF into the factory with the key he always carried with him. He turned on the one dim light that was still working. With a sense of relief he shut the door behind him and stood there in the absolute silence, staring at his machines. It was comforting just to be here, alone, away from everything.

On the cab ride over he had done nothing but go over and over in his mind the possibility that something could go wrong tomorrow. Was Elmer right? Was he a fool to try and pull this off? Would they have been smarter to have taken the incentive money and run with it?

No, Richie decided as he stood there, gaining back his sense of self. I worked too hard on this to let the good that it could bring slip away. Birdie and he had always stuck to the projects they started together, however disastrous the results. "It ain't over till it's over, right Richie?" he could hear her saying.

Richie walked over to his workbench. A couple of pairs of panty hose were draped over the side. I sure did make a lot of these, didn't I? he thought. He gathered them in his arms and held them against his cheek. A vast aching swept through him and he felt as empty and isolated as the factory. Tears stung his eyes and he made no attempt to stop them as they ran down his face. Birdie, he thought, I feel overwhelmed. He sat down and gently sobbed, feeling a release from all the pressure buildup and worry. All the work he'd done, and it would all be decided tomorrow. Even if everything turned out well, he knew it would be a letdown of sorts.

Listening to Lucille talk about getting home to her boyfriend had been especially poignant for him. I have a lot of friends, he thought as his chest heaved up and down, but I wish I had someone special who would be there all the time for me. Someone who I could take turns with getting out of bed in the morning to make the coffee, like I used to do with Birdie. Someone who would listen to my stories, however boring they got. Someone I could take care of.

Finally Richie wiped his eyes. Boy, am I a sad sack, he thought. I've come this far, I shouldn't fall down right before the finish line. I'll go over the list of names of the companies I wrote to. I want to recognize the people's names if they come to the cocktail party. He stood up and felt better. Maybe it was one of the big companies testing the panty hose. That would be great.

But as he walked over to the picnic table with his paperwork, he frowned, deep in thought. What was it that he hadn't tested these things for?

BARNEY FREIZE WAS back in his den, smoking his cigar, too excited to try to sleep. Ruth's secretary had finally called back and promised him he'd get the check tomorrow if everything worked out. Barney puffed. Tomorrow night I'll go out for a nice dinner, he thought. An occasional splurge was good for the soul. And if I get the big money, then it'll be time to make an appointment with my trusty travel agent. Europe, make room for Barney Freize.

I feel antsy, he thought. I can't just sit here, no matter how good this cigar is. He laughed aloud. If I'm going out for a big dinner tomorrow night, then I'd better work up my appetite. He went into the bedroom and got out his jogging suit. As he kicked off his Hush Puppies, he decided he'd run down by the beach. It would be soothing. After that he'd come home and sleep like a baby.

Judd Green watched Richie enter the front door of the factory. He pulled his car over to the side of the road where there were no streetlights. The area was deserted, which was a real bonus. He got out his phone and made a call.

Richie felt he had gone over his list long enough. We're going to have name tags anyway, he thought, but people like it when you know who they are.

As he gathered up the papers, the bench creaked. Boy, this place sure is making funny noises tonight, he thought. Either that or I have some imagination. But a few seconds later the sickening reality that he had not been imagining the noises hit him when the smell of smoke hit his nostrils and the sound of timber crackling filled his ears.

Out in the night air, Barney felt good. He ran along the beach and enjoyed the sounds of the waves breaking against the shore. When he looped around and started to head back toward his house, he decided he wasn't ready to go in yet. But what about a nice bath? he thought. These muscles are going to ache.

Wavering for a few minutes, he decided to stay out. It was a beautiful night. The bathtub would always be there. Before he knew it, his feet were taking him on the route he'd chosen that night, the route that led past the panty-hose factory. How appropriate, he thought. Maybe it'll be good luck. This is what started the whole adventure.

Barney turned down the long winding road that led to the factory. He thought he saw an orange glow in the distance, so he picked up his pace. What the hell is going on? he wondered.

With frightening speed, smoke filled the factory. Flames leapt up the walls and Richie ran with his panty hose to the front door. He tried to push it open but it wouldn't budge. This doesn't make sense, he thought frantically, there should be nothing blocking the door. He tried to run to the back, but flames had overtaken the rear of the building. Richie looked up and all the windows were barred.

I'm going to be fried, Richie thought. This is it. The smoke was getting thicker. He started to cough and ran for the front door again. It's my only chance, he thought. Through the barred window next to the door he could see out onto the dark street. I've got to get there. He screamed as he pounded and pushed on the door. "HELP ME! HELP!" But it was no use. The smoke was beginning to overcome him. He started to feel weak and thought that maybe he should just lie down.

With the panty hose in his hand, he started to slide down the door. Birdie's face filled his mind. "Get up, Richie," she seemed to be yelling. "It ain't over till it's over."

"But . . ."

"No buts, you've got a job to finish. Get up!"

Richie struggled to his feet and moved in front of the barred window. The flames leapt up behind him. He saw a lone figure standing out in the street watching the building. When the figure saw Richie, it ran up. To Richie, it was the most beautiful sight since he had first laid eyes on Birdie.

"Richie!" Barney Freize yelled. "What the hell are you doing in there?"

"Roasting marshmallows. What the hell do you think I'm doing? I can't get the front door open!"

Barney looked at the door. A Dumpster had been moved in front to block it. "Jesus Christ!" he yelled. "There's a Dumpster here. You push on the door and I'll try to pull it out of the way."

With all the strength Richie could muster, he threw his weight against the door, time after time, as Barney moved the Dumpster, inch by inch.

"Keep going, Richie," he could hear Barney yell through the roar of the fire behind him. Finally making enough progress to pry open the door a crack, Richie squeezed himself through and fell into the waiting arms of his former fellow maintenance worker, Barnard Thomas Freize.

"That's the punch line?" Joey asked Nadine incredulously.

"Wait a minute," she said. "I think I might have told it wrong."

"Helllllo, Nadine," he teased.

Regan laughed and looked at her watch. It was getting

late. "I hate to leave, but I'd better. I've got to get up early in the morning."

"You're not going on the stereo-shopping spree, are you?" Joey asked.

"No, I can't. We're leaving Nadine in charge of that one."

"I hope this guy has unlimited credit," Joey mumbled.

"Stop," Nadine protested. "Don't you worry, Regan. We'll get him the best buy in the Miami area."

"Nadine picked out the CD player for my car," Dennis said. "She did a great job."

"Thank you, Dennis."

"She fixed the one in my bedroom just this afternoon," Matt offered. "It took her about two minutes, and it had been broken for weeks. She stuck a wad of gum back there to keep the wire from coming out."

Joey looked at her. "Where'd you get the gum?"

"Found it."

He winked at Regan. "I wish they made a patch for gum chewers."

"I'll get Richie working on it," Regan said as she got up.

"We'll walk you home," Nadine said.

"That's okay," Regan replied.

"We insist," Joey pronounced. "This area is not the safest at night."

"Besides," Nadine said, "it's romantic to take a stroll in the evening, right, Joe?"

"You took the words right out of my mouth."

* * *

Regan climbed the stairs to her hotel room. Nadine and Joey are really nice, she thought. And they definitely belong together.

Inside the room Regan turned on the television. A long movie was just ending and the local news was coming up. She peeled off her clothes and threw them over the chair. Pulling an oversized T-shirt over her head, she went into the bathroom to wash her face and brush her teeth.

Five minutes later, she turned out the lights and got into bed. The sheets were crisp white cotton and felt fresh. She pushed the ''sleep'' button on the remote control so the television would automatically go off in thirty minutes. I just know I'll fall asleep with it on, she thought.

The news came on and there was the usual flurry of stories about local happenings. But when the announcer who looked like a surfer boy started to say, ''There was a fire tonight at a former panty-hose factory,'' Regan leaned forward and quickly turned up the volume.

Footage of the smoldering factory flashed on the screen as he reported, ''Arson is strongly suspected. It may even be a case of attempted murder, as a Dumpster had been used to block the front exit. Luckily no one was killed in the blaze, but a former factory worker, a Richard Blossom, is being treated at Miami General Hospital for smoke inhalation. Back to you, Barbara.''

''Richie!'' Regan wailed. She jumped out of bed and grabbed a pair of jeans. She stuffed her feet into her sneakers and pulled a light windbreaker off the hanger.

Within seconds she was out the door, hailing a cab, on her way to Miami General Hospital.

Richie lay stretched out on a bed in the emergency room of Miami General. Barney Freize was at his side.

"I feel much better now, Doctor," Richie was saying, "I really think you should let me go home."

Suddenly the doors swung open as a nurse tried to stop someone from charging in.

"Regan!" Richie called out happily. "I'm over here. It's all right," he said to the doctor, "she's my niece."

The doctor gave the nurse the signal to let her in.

"Richie, are you okay?" Regan said as she hurried over and bent down to kiss him.

"Good as new. Good as new. If this doctor would release me, I'd be even better."

"You shouldn't be alone tonight," the serious, young-looking doctor warned.

"I'll stay with him," Regan said.

"Isn't she a good niece?" Richie joked.

"He should be fine, but he needs to get some rest."

"I'll take care of it," Regan promised.

As Richie got out of bed he said, "By the way, Regan, meet Barney Freize. He saved my life tonight."

Regan and Richie had their taxi stop at Barney's house to drop him off.

"When I went out for a jog tonight," Barney joked, "I didn't know I was in for such an adventure."

"Thank God you like to exercise," Regan said. "Thank you so much."

"Yeah, thanks, Barn. I owe you one." Richie patted him on the back. "I've got a big weekend, but I'll call you and we'll have dinner next week." Barney started to get out of the cab. "Barn," Richie said.

Barney turned back. "Yeah, Rich."

Awkwardly Richie hugged him. "Thanks."

"You'd have done the same for me."

"That's true."

When they pulled away, Richie offered to stop at Regan's hotel to pick up a few things for her to spend the night.

"No way," Regan said. "I'm not letting you out of my sight tonight, not even to leave you waiting in the cab. I just want to get you home."

"Okay," Richie agreed. It was nice to be taken care of.

Barney Freize checked his answering machine. No messages. He opened the refrigerator and pulled out a beer. Sitting down at his kitchen table, the full effect of what had happened this evening began to dawn on him. Someone had tried to kill Richie. No two ways about it. But why? Did it have something to do with that panty hose? Am I responsible? he thought.

It was well after midnight, but he decided to call Danny. He needed to talk to him. As usual, he got his machine. But when the beep went off, Danny's tape must have started rewinding at high speed. It sounded like chipmunks on amphetamines.

Nothing could have prepared Barney for what he heard when Danny's messages started to play back. He knew he should have hung up, but it was as if the phone were Krazy-Glued to his ear.

"How's my Danny Wanny?" the familiar voice started to say in a juvenile tone. "Oh, Danny Boy, my scootchie-ootchie, we'll be together soon." Barney's face whitened. The last line of the message confirmed his worst fears. "Call back your wuving Ruthy Wu-thy."

His nephew was involved with the Calla-Lily woman. How deeply involved . . . ?

Back at the Fourth Quarter, Richie leaned on Regan as they walked up the steps to the second floor. It was late and everyone else had obviously gone to bed.

Inside the apartment, Regan asked, "Do you think a cup of tea would be good before you went to sleep?"

"Great idea. I guess nobody knows what happened yet, huh, Regan. There are no messages on the answering machine."

"I caught it on the Late News. I think everybody must have already been in bed."

"Boy, are they going to be surprised."

"To say the least," Regan said as she filled the kettle and turned on the gas.

"Someone's out to get me, do you think, Regan?"

"Unless that Dumpster moved itself in front of the door."

"You know what this means, don't you?" Richie asked happily. "Somebody must like my panty hose! They think it's good enough to kill me for."

"Don't even joke about it, Richie," Regan said as

she brought the teacups, milk and sugar out to the coffee table in front of the couch, where Richie was sitting. The kettle started whistling angrily, a piercing, shrill sound that instantly set Regan's teeth on edge.

"That kettle would wake the dead," Richie remarked.

"Kettle? What kettle?" Regan asked as she hurried into the kitchen and yanked it off the stove.

"I like your sense of humor, Regan. It's important to have one."

"I agree, Richie," Regan said as she poured the hot water into the cups. "Life would be pretty tough without it."

Companionably they sat and sipped their tea. Regan noticed Richie's eyes grow heavy.

"We'd better get some rest. It's late. I'll just stretch out on the couch here."

"It pulls out," Richie enthused.

"It does?"

"It's a Castro Convertible. Birdie and I used to get such a kick watching that little Bernadette Castro pull apart those couches on the TV commercials. Come to think of it, we could have used her help tonight getting that Dumpster to budge."

"She's running the company now," Regan informed him. "And she does her own radio commercials on 'Imus in the Morning' in New York. Last time I was home I heard Imus yelling at her for dragging him to some boring luncheon."

Richie shook his head. "It's still hard to think of her

as all grown up. Boy, time does fly, huh, Regan?'' he asked as he got up and yawned.

"It sure does," Regan agreed. "And before you know it, it's going to be morning and that phone's going to start ringing, with everyone calling to make sure you're okay."

"That's nice," Richie said as he started for the bedroom.

Regan pulled the cushions off the couch. "Yes, it is," she said quietly.

AT DAYBREAK, A sliver of orange sun peeked over the horizon in the mountains of Colorado. The campsite of the Wild West Tour group was peaceful. All eight members of the posse, as they liked to call themselves, snuggled in their sleeping bags around the embers from last night's campfire. Preston Landers pulled his special-issue sleeping bag around his slight frame as he dreamed about the storytelling session that had taken place around the campfire just hours before.

As was their ritual each evening, one person led the group with stories about his boyhood. Last night had been Preston's turn.

He'd told them about his privileged life in New York City where his family's Fifth Avenue apartment overlooked Central Park. He'd hated it. All he wanted to be was a cowboy, out branding cattle, sleeping under the stars. A trip to a dude ranch when he was seven years old reinforced that ardent desire.

His family had tried to placate him by sending him out every Saturday, cowboy hat in place, into the wilds of Central Park with his nanny, who watched him go round and round riding a purple horse on the carousel, firing at her with his pop gun every 360 degrees. But somehow it just wasn't enough.

He had wanted to go to high school out in Wyoming on a special exchange program. Instead he was sent to a prep school in New Jersey. They didn't ride herd there, they rode to hounds. It had been a bitter disappointment.

Time slipped away, Preston recounted, and before he knew it he was caught up in the rat race, making money in business, his childhood dream buried but not forgotten. Until now.

He hoped he hadn't bored the group too much. He'd gone on a little longer than usual and a couple of the guys had lain back in their sleeping bags during his soliloquy, never regaining consciousness for the singing of "Taps," a ceremony that capped off each evening.

The air at this hour of the morning was fresh and crisp, with a slight nip to it. The occasional sounds of nature gently cut through the stillness, making it a perfect spot to film, say, a cornflakes commercial.

But in one brief moment it all ended. The mules started to bray wildly. Dust started to blow over the campsite. Preston Landers's peaceful slumber communing with nature in the great outdoors was rudely interrupted by the roar of a helicopter as it settled down in a nearby clearing. With a sinking heart he looked up and saw the Calla-Lily logo on its side and knew that, for whatever reason, his vacation was over.

With much grumbling, Preston pulled on his Levi's 501 jeans bought especially for the trip and packed up his vagabond stove, buddy burner, multipurpose pocket knife and video camera. He planned to put together a tape of the journey, set it to country music, and sell it to the other campers.

"Did everyone fill out their order forms for *High Noon Two*?" he asked his fellow ramblers as he rolled up his sleeping bag and tied it with a knot.

Most of them grunted, "Yeah, partner" as they rubbed the sleep from their eyes.

"You can send me your checks and self-addressed stamped envelopes when I've got it ready."

His gear in tow, Preston walked over and patted the heads of the mules. The one he had christened Ruth stared blankly at him and blinked.

"I wish I could take you with me," Preston whispered. "But where I'm going there's only room for one Ruth. And you wouldn't want to be there."

Preston boarded *Calla-Lily I*, strapped himself in, and waved good-bye to the Wild West Tour as the helicopter lifted him toward the heavens on his way back to the boardrooms of America.

REGAN WOKE UP to the delicious smell of fresh-brewed coffee. Surprisingly she'd fallen into a heavy sleep and had slept for a solid six hours. She heard Richie puttering around in the kitchen.

"Richie," she called out.

"Good morning, honey. I'll be right there."

Regan sat up in bed and watched as Richie carried in a tray with coffee, juice and bagels.

"What service!" Regan said as she gratefully accepted a cup of coffee. "I'm supposed to be looking after you."

"Eh," Richie muttered. "I heated up the bagels because they're from yesterday. You have to eat them quick before they get hard again."

Regan laughed. "Thanks. How do you feel this morning?"

"I have a little case of opening-night jitters, but other than that, I'm grateful to be alive."

The phone rang.

Regan raised an eyebrow. "Here we go." She sipped her coffee as Richie settled himself in the chair next to the phone.

"I'm fine, I'm fine," he said to the caller. "Regan, it's Bridget and Ed . . . huh . . . Regan heard it on the news last night and came to get me at the hospital . . . she stayed over . . . We don't know who tried to kill me . . . Don't worry about it . . . I'll see you later."

Richie hung up and smiled. "Everybody's a wreck."

The phone rang again. "Richie Blossom here," he answered. "Nora, love. I feel fine. Your daughter is here making sure I don't get into any more trouble . . . I'll put you on the speakerphone . . ."

"Regan?" Nora asked.

"Hi, Mom." Regan leaned back against her propped-up pillow.

"You both are okay?"

"Fine," they said in unison.

"Well, I've got some exciting news."

Richie leaned into the phone. "What's that, love?"

"Not only have we gotten a lot more responses from people who want to come to the party, but someone very important and influential and rich called to see if he would be welcome."

'WHO?" Richie yelled and spilled a few drops of coffee on his bathrobe. "Don't keep us in suspense!"

"She can't help it. That's her business," Regan remarked.

Nora paused and pronounced his name with emphasis. "Dayton Rotter."

"Dayton Rotter?" Richie repeated. "Dayton Rotter!"

"Wow!" Regan said. "He's really coming?"

"Yes," Nora said with satisfaction. "He heard about it from the models. Your father and I are doing our best to make sure the word spreads that he'll be there. I have to call the manager, Nick, and let him know."

"You better hurry up," Regan advised. "He's going out this morning on a hunt for a stereo."

"Dayton Rotter?" Richie said almost to himself. "I guess I'm in the big time now!"

There was a knock at the door.

"Excuse me, Nora, I have to answer the door."

"Sure, Richie. Regan," Nora asked, "do you want to come to the hotel this morning and we'll go over to the luncheon together?"

"Yes, but we can't stay too long," Regan said.

"We won't. Why don't you come by around ten forty-five?"

"Okay, Mom. I'll see you later."

Richie, followed by Lucille, hurried to turn off the speakerphone. "Lucille, sit down."

"Richie, I got so worried when I heard the news this morning. Hi, Regan. Sorry to barge in like this."

"Not at all. I've got to get going, anyway." Richie had lent her Birdie's old bathrobe. She went into the other room to get dressed. When she came back out, she folded up the Bernadette Castro Special and picked the cushions off the floor.

"Now, Richie, you do promise to stay here this morning and not go out alone."

"I promise, Regan."

"We're all going to bus up to the Watergreen together for the fashion show early this afternoon. Richie, you're going to come with us, aren't you?" Lucille asked.

"The Fourth Quarter contingent will proceed together," Richie said excitedly.

Regan looked at him. "There's not going to be a lot of time for me to come back and get you. If you go with them, Richie, please stay with them. I want to get you through today safely."

"No problem," Richie smiled.

"I'll keep my eye on him," Lucille assured her. "I'm very good at that."

IRVING FRANKLIN STIRRED at his work station. He lifted his head off the Formica countertop where he had been wrestling with the panty hose the night before. The big clock on the wall with the second hand he needed to time certain experiments precisely read eight-seventeen.

Fern should be coming down in a few minutes to check on me, he thought groggily. I can't believe I fell asleep. I just put my head down to rest my eyes an hour ago. Just before he fell asleep, as a final test he'd added dollops of the ridiculously expensive new cream that his daughter had insisted on buying just yesterday.

Uh, he thought. This place stinks. He walked over to the Crockpot that was really intended for the delicate slow cooking of meats and vegetables, not lingerie. He picked up the lid. Stew au hose. Good enough to drive Ruth crazy.

A quick examination of the specimen in question revealed that, indeed, it was as good as new.

Irving sighed. That's all, folks, he thought. I've done everything I can think of to make this stuff unravel, one way or the other. But it couldn't be done.

Disgusted, he dropped the hose back in the Crockpot, straightened up the counter, and started up the steps, ignoring the nagging little voice that told him to take one more look. He needed a shower and a change of clothes before he headed over to Ruthy Wuthy to break the bad news.

Thank God she can't take it out on me, he thought. What a shock it had been when he wandered down to his lab during the company Christmas party and found her experimenting with the gardener, who was calling her Ruthy Wuthy. Ruthy had looked up just as he snapped their picture.

BARNEY FREIZE HAD had a terrible night's sleep. He was still in shock over Ruth's message on Danny's answering machine. To think that those two were involved was bad enough, but what were they up to? Something told him he should not have brought those panty hose to Calla-Lily. And now Richie's life was in danger, probably thanks to him.

He paced around his little house. The best thing he could do was just to go and talk to Danny. That's it. Danny had never returned Barney's call but he probably got home late. The question was, from where? And God knew, that machine of his couldn't be depended upon to deliver the messages. At least not to Danny.

Barney grabbed his car keys and hurried out the door. It took him exactly eight minutes to reach Danny's neighborhood. He pulled his sedan into the driveway and turned off the car. It was still early, but he couldn't wait. Charging up to the door, he rang the bell and waited.

A few minutes later, a sleepy-looking Danny answered the door.

"Uncle Barney, what are you doing here?"

"We need to talk."

"Come on in."

Barney followed him into the kitchen. He cringed when he saw a can of turpentine on the counter.

"I tried to call you last night."

"I didn't get the message. My answering machine is screwing up a little bit."

"I know."

"How do you know?"

"Let's just say I thought I had reached the hallway outside a newborn nursery, scootchie-ootchie."

Danny's face reddened. "That's none of your business."

"What did you do last night?" Barney asked.

"I painted a friend's apartment. Why are you asking me these questions?" Danny asked, annoyed.

"What's the turpentine doing here?"

"To get the paint off my hands. What do you think?"

"You know, Danny, in Florida people can go to jail for a long time for attempted murder."

"What are you talking about?"

"You don't know?"

"Of course not."

"Then tell me about your wonderful plans to be with Ruthy Wuthy."

JOEY HONKED THE horn of his car. "Nadine, hurry up! I'm going to be late for work."

"Hold your horses, I'm coming," Nadine said as she struggled out the front door, her purse dangling in one hand, a cup of coffee in the other. She handed the cup to Joey to hold while she got in the car and buckled her seat belt. "Ready," she pronounced.

"Well, hallelujah," Joey said as they drove off.

Nadine raised her eyebrows. "That'd be a good CD to buy for the fashion show." She started to sing, "Hal-le-lu-jah, hal-le-lu-jah, hal-le-lu-jah, hal-le-lu-jah . . ."

Joey switched on the radio.

"Are you trying to give me some sort of message here?" Nadine asked.

"Who, me?"

"Yeah, you. Unless there's somebody in the backseat I don't know about."

"I love the sound of your voice, you know that." He patted her thigh. "But not your singing voice."

Nadine appeared nonplussed. "Nobody's perfect." She took a sip of the coffee that was sloshing around in the wide-brimmed cup.

"So, you know which stores you're going to take this clown to?" Joey asked.

"Uh-huh. Do you want to come over to the fashion show?"

"Sure. I hope that Richie guy can pull this off."

"Me too. I'll go back with Nick and help him set up the stereo, so why don't you come to the hotel when you're finished working?"

"Okay. That should be early afternoon." Joey paused. "If my boss only knew what the people from the Fourth Quarter are doing to hang on to that place . . ."

"Don't tell him. He wouldn't be too happy to find out that the commission check he's probably planning for the Golden Sun could be a lot skinnier."

"My lips are sealed."

They drove along, with Nadine flipping stations after every song.

"God forbid we should hear any news," Joey muttered.

"Buy a paper," Nadine suggested as she threw her drained coffee cup on the floor of the backseat. "It's got a big handle. It shouldn't roll around too much."

"Thank you for caring."

Finally, Joey pulled up the hill of the Watergreen's horseshoe-shaped driveway. He leaned over to kiss her. "Now don't run away with this guy."

"You never know." Nadine kissed him back. "He might like my singing."

She stepped inside the lobby of the Watergreen and was impressed by the beautiful view of the ocean from the huge windows on the opposite wall. The blue water sparkled under the brilliant sunshine. Not bad, she thought. I'll have to get Joey to take me here for a drink some night.

There was a bustle in the air. People with notebooks and pens were scurrying around. Nadine hurried over to the elevator. As she waited she studied the two signs, side by side, that listed the convention seminars for the day. The first one read: " 'Panty Hose in a Glass—Efforts to Make Our Packaging Recyclable,' Room 120A; 'The "INGS" of Panty Hose Production—Knitting, Weaving, Dyeing,' Room 124; 'Panty Hose for the Funky Crowd—Jeweled, Studded, Crazy—Cost of Production vs. Profit,' Room 126." Hmmm, Nadine thought. Things that I never lost sleep over.

The other sign read: " 'Ashes to Ashes—Cremation vs. Burial,' Room 112; 'Keeping Up Employee Morale Around the Home,' Room 116; 'The Latest Models of the Six-Foot Bungalow—Coffins on Display,' Banquet Room B." How cheerful, Nadine mused.

The elevator bell donged and the doors opened. Nadine pressed "PH" and was whisked up to the top floor of the Watergreen. Around the corner and down the hall were the double doors that opened into Nick Fargus's suite. One of them was partially ajar. Nadine knocked on it. "Hello."

Nick hurriedly opened the door. A valet stood next to him in the foyer, a hanger holding a flowered shirt in a dry cleaner's bag resting on his index finger. "Nadine?" Nick asked.

"Since birth."

"Come on in. I'm Nick." He turned to the valet. "Did you get out the stains?"

"We tried very hard, Mr. Fargus. There's still one little smidgen of tomato sauce, but I really think it blends in with the flowers."

Nick looked at him sternly. "Very well."

"Next time put some club soda on it right away," Nadine suggested.

The valet exited with a downcast look on his face. With all the stains they got out for all the people who only visited the Watergreen once, it was just such bad luck that they couldn't do it for the boss, he thought.

"Come on inside, Nadine. Take a look at the view," he said proudly, leading her to the windows.

"Nice place you got here," Nadine commented as she followed him in. "You've got a runway set up, I see?"

"A couple of the guys came up and built it last night. You like it?"

"Very professional. The view is great too. What a bachelor pad."

Nick's face lit up. "You think so?"

"Heck, yeah. I'm glad my boyfriend doesn't live in a place like this. As it is now, if he ever brought another girl home, she'd trip and break her neck right inside his front door. You don't have a girlfriend?"

"No. You really think this is a good place to have the party?"

"It's a great place. What are you worried about?"

"Nothing. Where should we put the stereo?"

Nadine looked around. "Now let's see. It depends on the system we get. How much do you want to spend?"

Nick shrugged his shoulders. "How much do you think I should spend?"

"You plan to live here for a while?"

He managed a little laugh. "Unless I get fired."

"That'd be a bummer." Nadine walked around the large room. "Let's see. Do you want to put speakers in the bedroom?"

Nick shook his head. "Uh-huh. The models are going to change in there."

"Lucky you."

Nick grinned. "I know."

"Ohhh, so you're looking forward to having the models here, huh?" Nadine teased.

He shuffled his feet, embarrassed. "It'll be fun. You think they'll like the runway?"

"They'll love the whole place," Nadine assured him.

The phone rang. His manner became efficient as he picked it up. "Nick Fargus."

Nadine sat down on the couch.

". . . more acceptances, that's fine. I'll let the banquet manager know . . . the more the merrier . . . who else? . . ."

Nadine watched as the expression on Nick's face clouded and he practically squealed.

". . . Dayton Rotter is coming? . . . No, of course, that's great . . . see you later." He hung up the phone looking dejected.

"The competition is coming?" Nadine asked.

"Huh? Oh. I don't care," Nick protested weakly.

"He's just another good-looking guy," Nadine said with forced cheerfulness.

"Who also happens to be rich and famous!" Nick blurted.

"Forget it, Nick. You're going to have a good time today. Just be yourself. You're the host! He's not going to tie up everyone's attention the whole time."

"I guess so."

"Let's get out of here and buy a stereo that's going to make this place rock!"

"Okay. Now, how much do you think I'm going to have to spend?" he asked as the door closed behind them.

JUDD GREEN SAT in the phone booth out by the pool bar. The bar was closed and there were only a couple of bathers sunning themselves at the other end of the pool. It was still early.

"You poured it! You saw the door was blocked! You saw him through the window! How was I supposed to know somebody was going to take a jog in the boonies late at night?"

He played with his mirror sunglasses as he listened. "I know how bad it is. I know you're getting the pressure. Believe me, I wish this job was finished. Although it should have been taken care of a long time ago . . . Listen, the funeral convention ends early this afternoon. I know what we can do. We'll need a legitimate-looking business van. Get two of the guys in workers' uniforms . . .''

Someone tapped on the window of the phone booth. ''Are you going to be finished soon?'' a woman in a skirted bathing suit asked.

Judd turned to her and opened the door. Trying to keep his tone civil, he said, ''I'll be out in a few minutes.''

Hurriedly he explained the rest of his plan as the bather wandered off. ''I tell you, it's going to work. We'll go straight to the dock. At the party, I'll concentrate on the old guy. You take care of Regan Reilly.''

IT WAS NOT just a gray haze of smoke that hung in the air of the Calla-Lily suite. The atmosphere was thick with the kind of tension you could cut with a knife.

"This waiting is killing me!" Ruth screamed as she puffed her twenty-seventh cigarette of the day.

The Calla-Lily board members sat on the couches looking glum. They had all arrived at 7 A.M., at the precise time that the cowpoke was spotted in the wilds of Colorado. While he was jetting back across the country, they were made to sit and discuss with Ruth, if "discuss" was the right word, Calla-Lily's final decision on purchasing the Birdie Panty Hose.

"To buy, or not to buy, that is the question," one of them had made the mistake of joking as he held up a glazed doughnut in the air for emphasis. The force of

Ruth's reaction had startled him so much that he dropped the doughnut in his cup of coffee.

The doorbell rang. Ethel, back in the salt mines, answered the door.

It was Irving Franklin. Late as usual.

"I don't know how he gets away with it," one of the board members muttered as he bit into a crumb bun that broke apart, dusting his suit with confectioners sugar.

"Good morning, everyone."

"Would you like some coffee?" Ethel asked.

"Thank you, Ethel. Yes, I would. Black."

Like Ruth's mood, Ethel thought. Easy to remember.

Irving sat down. He looked over at Ruth and smiled. "Good morning, Ruth."

"What's the deal, Irving?" she responded.

Ethel placed a coffee cup in front of Irving. "Ruth?" she asked.

"Is it important, Ethel?" Ruth demanded to know.

"I was just thinking that I'd run downstairs and get those papers you wanted photocopied . . ." Her voice trailed off. Before this place explodes, she wanted to add.

"Go."

"Thank you."

Irving sipped his drink. "Good coffee." He cleared his throat. "I guess you can tell that I did not come in here jumping with joy. I was up all night determined to find something wrong with that panty hose. I cooked it, beat it, washed it, stomped on it. I'm sorry. It *seems* to be just perfect."

An animal-like moan emanated from Ruth's throat.

"We've got to buy it! That idiot better get back here soon and sign his consent!"

The board members shook their heads, agreeing that indeed the best thing was to fork over the money.

Three minutes later the door to the suite flung open. Ethel was back, the papers in her hand yet to be copied. She could tell that the news from Irving had not been good. And now she had more bad news that she couldn't wait to tell Ruth.

"I thought you'd want to know . . . I was just down in the manager's office. The buzz is that Dayton Rotter is coming to the cocktail party. He's very interested in buying the Birdie Panty Hose . . ."

The last thing Ruth saw before she fainted was the vision of Grandpa pointing his finger at her, shouting, "You ruined my company!"

A T TABLES SET around the poolside in the back-yard of the home of the Durkin family's good friends, Dina and Sean Clancy, fourteen women had gathered for Maura's bridesmaids' brunch. Regan and Nora joined the five other bridesmaids, Maura, Bridget, Dina, and a handful of other female relatives of Maura's and John's for the traditional hen party.

Colorful floral centerpieces adorned the tables, which were shaded by large yellow umbrellas. Small boxes with pale-pink wrapping and gold bows were waiting at the places assigned to the bridesmaids. A bouquet of balloons was tied to the buffet table, which would soon be filled with quiches and salads.

"What's John doing today?" Regan asked Maura as she sipped a tall glass of fresh-squeezed orange juice.

"Golfing. He figured he could get in eighteen holes before he took care of some minor last-minute errands like picking up the rings, the marriage license, and his tux."

"At least he's not the nervous type."

"He said I've been doing enough worrying for both of us lately."

"Just think, Maura, tomorrow night you'll be on your way, and everything will be all behind you."

"I hope so, Regan." Maura's look turned serious. "After what happened last night with Richie, I feel so sure that something else bad is going to happen."

Regan tried to conceal her worry. "If Richie manages to sell his panty hose this afternoon, he'll be the happiest guy in Florida."

"I hope so. He's had so many of these inventions before that have never worked out. We thought it was more a hobby for him than anything. But now everyone seems to think he's come across something that will really fly. Which could be dangerous. Do you know how many people have been paid to keep their inventions off the market?"

"I've heard of a few."

"Well, could it be that whoever blocked Richie in that factory last night didn't want to have to write the check?"

"I don't know, Maura. But we're keeping an eye on Richie today, and hopefully after the fashion show the panty hose will be someone else's worry."

"I wish I could come to that, Regan, but I'm not

completely packed and we have the rehearsal dinner tonight . . .''

"Don't worry about it. We're going to see you later anyway.''

"Will everyone please help themselves?'' Dina urged the group as she carried out two large dishes of quiche, fresh from the oven.

After dessert and coffee, Regan thanked Maura again for the pearl-and-sapphire earrings the bridesmaids would all be wearing the next day, and she and Nora hurried back to the Watergreen.

L IKE AN OLD pro, Nadine wandered up and down the aisles of Dobb's Stereo Store studying the CD players. Nick was close at her heels, looking slightly baffled.

"I want one that looks really good," he insisted.

Nadine held her finger to her lip and tapped it. "Right. Now, the woofers and the tweeters . . ."

"The what?" Nick asked.

"The woofers and the tweeters. Don't you know what they are?"

"Oh, sure, yeah, the woofers and the tweeters. Of course."

Nadine stopped and smiled at him. "What are they then?"

Nick gestured with his hand. "Parts of the stereo."

"The loudspeakers, Nick." Nadine started to move on. "You know, you don't have to pretend so much."

"Do you think I do that?" Nick asked quickly.

"Uh-huh," Nadine said as she checked a price tag. "You're too anxious, too worried about what people think. And people are going to think what they're going to think, so there's no use trying to control it."

"I don't do that," Nick protested.

"Yes, you do. Why else would you be agonizing about whether or not to wear that flowered shirt today?"

"I just asked your opinion."

"Three times. Wear what you want to wear and forget everybody else if they can't take a joke."

Nick followed her into the next aisle. "You think there's something wrong with me?"

"No. But I wish you would chill out and just let things happen. I get the feeling that impressing the models today is the most important thing in the world to you."

"I'm proud of the Watergreen Hotel and want to restore it to its former glory as the spot to be in Miami."

"No, you don't. You just want to date the models. Here we go," Nadine said. "For what you want to spend, this stereo here is the best buy. It looks good, has great sound, has an AM/FM radio and a tape deck besides a CD player, and it's in your price range. What do you say?"

"Fine."

"And we'll get you some of those woofers and tweeters for your bedroom too."

"Sounds kinky."

"There you go. Now let's find someone who can get this order moving."

After they had packed the car with the stereo boxes, Nick and Nadine hurried into the music store to pick up the CDs Regan had requested for the fashion show. Nadine bought a few extra ones for Joey and, after less deliberation than usual, Nick made a purchase that was the official start of his CD collection.

"Well, what do you know," Nadine said as they got back into the car and pulled out of the parking lot. "It's almost show time."

WHEN REGAN AND Nora got to Nick Fargus's suite, they stepped into a flurry of activity. Room-service waiters were setting up the bar and the hors d'oeuvres. A maid was retouching the windows, making sure that they sparkled. Flowers were being delivered.

Nadine stepped out of the bedroom, holding a hammer. "Hi, Regan!"

"Hi, Nadine. This is my mother—"

"Mrs. Reilly, I love your books. Regan, you didn't tell me your mother was the one who wrote those books that keep me up all night."

Nora laughed. "As long as they don't put you to sleep."

"No way. When I was reading the last one I got so scared that I got out of bed to make double sure the door

261

was locked. The next day at work I had to go out to my car at lunchtime to take a nap.''

"Hi, everybody,'' Nick said, emerging from the bathroom in his flowered shirt. He was feeling proud of himself, having left out for the models everything he thought they might need, including his new skin cream.

"All set?'' Regan asked.

"Nadine's in charge. She's got the stereo all set up. We were just going to put in our first CD.'' He laughed. "She also told me to put a sign on the bathroom door telling people that there's another bathroom one flight down in the health club.''

Nadine said matter-of-factly, "You've got over a hundred people in here drinking and one bathroom? The one in your bedroom will be off limits because the models will be in and out of there. People come for one drink and they stay for another and before you know it you've got a line.''

"I'll get out my Magic Marker,'' Nick promised.

"Speaking of that, Regan, we'd better write up the rest of the name tags for the people who just called in,'' Nora said.

"Hello, hello, hello,'' Richie called as he led the Fourth Quarter contingent into the suite.

"This is a good place for a party,'' Flo remarked.

"Beautiful,'' Lucille murmured.

Nick went over and shook Richie's hand. "Good to see you, Richie. And who do we have here?''

"The models!''

When Nick tried to speak, his voice had a croaky quality. "The models?''

"Yes. Say hello to Flo and Bessie and Pearl and—"

"We've been doing nothing but practicing our strut," Pearl reported.

"Great," Nick forced himself to say. "I thought you were from South Beach."

"We are, honey," Flo said as she walked past him to check out the view.

Nick hoped his disappointment didn't show, then realized Nadine was watching him. *You're too anxious. Just let things happen.* "Well, you all look terrific," he said heartily.

Nadine winked at him.

"We do have a few spring chickens coming up from one of the agencies," Richie explained. "They should be here in a few minutes."

Nick's spirits brightened. I don't have to feel guilty that I'm glad, he thought.

L UKE RUBBED HIS eyes. It had been a long morning, but the business end of the convention was coming to a close. All in all, it had been worthwhile. He had met with suppliers, gone to some of the seminars, hooked up with old friends from the business, and given a successful speech.

Now it was past noon and people were heading to lunch dates or out to the pool to take advantage of the beautiful weather. But Luke wanted to take one more look at the coffin display. He'd seen a few models that were interesting. They cost less and he could pass on those savings to his customers.

He walked down the carpeted hallway toward the display room. Everything was quiet. The large room was off the beaten path, away from the hubbub of the hotel lobby. He pulled open the door and stepped inside, alone in the room with rows of coffins. No matter how long I last in this business, he thought, I don't think I'll ever get totally immune to the sight of these things.

After jotting down the information he needed about several different makes, he put his pen away and looked around one final time. They'll be coming sometime this afternoon to haul these out of here, he thought. But after the problems of bringing them in the other day, the only way the management was going to let them be carried out was via the rear exit.

Back in the hotel lobby he headed toward the main bar. He was meeting Ed for a quick sandwich and then they were going upstairs to meet Nora and Bridget at the fashion show. And after that, he thought, who knows. Hopefully a little time to relax.

THE CALLA-LILY private jet touched down at Miami International Airport. When it finally came to a stop, the door was opened and Preston Landers was greeted with a blast of hot, sticky air.

"Now damn it!" he mumbled. "Where I just came from, the air was nice and cool." The flight attendant looked at him sympathetically.

"Have a good day, sir," she said as he stepped off the plane.

"I doubt it," he replied.

Down on the tarmac a limousine was waiting to whisk him to the Watergreen Hotel.

"We have to hurry, sir," the driver said as he held the door open for him. "They're waiting for you at the hotel. They've called several times to see if you'd landed yet.''

Preston kicked some mud off his cowboy boots. ''I guess they'll just have to wait a little longer.''

"Yes, sir.'' The driver shut the door behind Preston, ran around the side of the car, jumped in and screeched off.

Ruth was propped on a couch in the Calla-Lily suite. She was furious at herself for fainting in front of this bunch. It was just that the news about Dayton Rotter had been such a mortal blow. It made her all the more convinced that they had to get the check into that Richie Blossom's hands, and get it there soon. Thanks to Nora Regan Reilly, the cocktail party and fashion show had become a hot topic. See if I ever buy another one of her books, Ruth thought.

"WHERE IS THAT IDIOT?'' she screamed.

"Ruth, calm yourself,'' Ethel urged.

"Calm myself? How can I calm myself? My whole life is passing before my eyes and you tell me to calm myself!''

"He's on his way.''

"What is he doing, riding a pony in from the airport?''

There was a knock at the door.

"Thank God!'' Ruth screamed and ran to answer it. She yanked it open to find Barney Freize staring her in the face.

"I've come to pick up my check."

Ruth turned away, dismissing him. "I can't worry about that right now!"

"Well, Ruthy Wuthy, I think you'd better."

Irving fired a glance at Ruth before she flung back around.

"I think I'd like to come in and perhaps have a cup of tea," Barney said.

Irving jumped up. "I'm Irving Franklin, the engineer." He gestured for Barney to sit next to him as the other board members watched in astonishment. "Please join us. Won't you?" He smiled at Ruth, who for the first time in her life was left speechless.

Nora stood at the doorway greeting members of the National Panty-Hose Association. Some of them had indeed brought books for her to sign, and as she was busy writing "Happy Birthday" or "Best Wishes," she was aware of Richie pacing around nervously.

"You ought to write a book about a panty-hose convention," one of the guests told her.

"Maybe I will," Nora laughed.

"We've got some good stories," the woman chuckled. "Give me a call if you ever need any material."

As the guests floated in they accepted drinks and hors d'oeuvres from the passing waiters. A few wandered out on the terrace to appreciate the view fully.

All the models were waiting in the bedroom, dressed in their panty hose, ready to go. Nick was busy playing host, running in and out with drink orders. Nadine had the stereo going, playing lively energetic music, but at Nora's request kept it at a low-enough level so that people could hear each other talk.

Judd Green came up in the elevator with several other people, and when they stopped to get their name tags, he was happy to see that there were some blank tags left on the table for guests to fill in. For us bad guys, he thought as he wrote LOWELL EVANS in block letters.

Slipping past Nora without saying hello he went over to the bar and ordered a Bloody Mary. He looked around and saw the Blossom guy talking to a girl at the stereo. I'm going to have to get him out of here during the fashion show, he thought. He had a plan that he thought would work. It had to.

The traffic coming from the airport was terrible. Preston rested his head back against the seat and was philosophical.

"This morning when I woke up, my head was pressed to Mother Earth. The cawing of whatever bird it was up in the sky was music to my ears. I realized on this trip that the pursuit of money is something I should have given up a long time ago."

"Oh, someone broke down in the middle lane, that's our problem," the driver said nervously, concentrating on the road.

"Yup. My happiness was out on the trails with a mule I called Ruth."

The driver looked in the rearview mirror. "You want to call Ruth?" he asked quickly.

"I'd like to," Preston said with a tear in his eye,

"but I'm afraid she'd be a little hard to reach. The poor thing is probably struggling right now without me there on her back, my legs wrapped around her, patting her, tickling her, giving her encouragement."

The driver's eyes nearly popped out of his head. I was told it was company policy not to date anyone else at Calla-Lily, he thought.

Regan stood in the corner talking to Nadine, Joey and Scott. The guys had come over together after Joey finished work.

"I've got to see how my girls do," Scott smiled. "I want to find out if you're paying them too much."

"Ha-ha," Nadine said. "This is for a good cause."

Outside in the hallway Nora surveyed the few name tags left unclaimed.

"How are you doing, Richie?" she asked when he stepped out the door.

"The place is crowded, isn't it, Nora?"

"It sure is. Are you nervous?"

"Yes."

Nora smiled at him. "Keep the faith. Oh, good. Here come Luke and Ed and Bridget."

"We met in the elevator," Bridget said exuberantly. When she stepped in the doorway she added, "It looks like you have a sold-out show."

"Let's hope they're the right audience!" Richie exclaimed. "Nora, when do you think we should start?"

"Dayton Rotter hasn't gotten here yet."

"Then by all means let's wait."

Ruth deliberately kept a general discussion going, not wanting people to break into private conversations. The last thing she needed was to have Irving and Barney talk. Irving was a troublemaker and she couldn't stand the thought of him having any more power over her. It was bad enough he had those pictures of her and Danny from the Christmas party. When the doorbell rang, Ruth practically ejected from her seat. This time she found Preston Landers standing there clad in his boots and spurs, cowboy hat, plaid shirt, and fringed vest. He was twirling a lasso and was munching chewing tobacco.

"Howdy, partner," was his greeting.

"YOU!" Ruth practically lunged at him. "Get in here!"

"Whoa. Down girl, down girl," he said as he swaggered into the boardroom to the total astonishment of his colleagues. He tipped his hat. "Howdy."

"Howdy," they all mumbled self-consciously.

Ruth threw a piece of paper at him. "SIGN THIS!"

"I've got to look over the fine print here, ma'am . . ." he said, but Ethel interrupted, covering the mouthpiece of the phone with her hand.

"Excuse me, Ruth,"—Ethel braced herself—"but Dayton Rotter just pulled in downstairs."

"SIGN! SIGN! SIGN!" By now Ruth was jumping up and down.

Preston submitted, scrawling his name, and before he could finish saying "Here's my John Hancock," Ruth had flown out the door, with Ethel, Irving, Barney and the Calla-Lily board members in hot pursuit.

NORA GLANCED AT her watch. It was five past three. "It looks like everybody's having a good time, but we shouldn't keep them waiting too much longer," she told Richie. "Dayton Rotter might not even show up."

"You're right, Nora."

"If he's not here by three-fifteen, I'll give them a little welcoming speech to try and stall for a few more minutes . . ."

"She's got the gift of gab, Richie," Luke said soothingly. "Dayton Rotter will get here before she finishes telling everybody how thrilled she is to see them."

Richie watched Nora thread her way through the crowd to whisper something in Nadine's ear. He could tell Nora was telling Nadine when to lower the music so she could start her speech. Then Nora joined a cluster of people on the terrace.

"I'm too nervous to stay here," Richie moaned. "I might get sick or something. I'll give the girls a pep talk and then I'm gonna stand by the door. I don't want to faint or anything."

Luke watched sympathetically as Richie bolted down the hall to the bedroom door, followed by the young fellow who'd been introduced as Scott. He had something to do with the modeling agency, Luke thought.

Richie was about to tap on the bedroom door when he felt a hand on his arm. He jumped. "What?" Then he said sheepishly, "Gee-whiz, Scott, I'm a bundle of nerves, I guess. I didn't realize you were there."

"Richie, I finally get you alone. I have to talk to you."

"Gee, Scott. Can't it wait?"

"I wish it could. Richie, one of the biggest movie producers saw your commercial. He thought it was great. He's casting a movie that he thinks you might be perfect for. But he needs a special picture of you right away. His photographer is standing by at the elevator."

"Me in a movie? You need a picture? What about the stack of pictures you already got of me? I paid plenty to have those done."

"Richie, they're not right for this." Scott's face was inches from his. "Richie, trust me. Why do you think I'm in this business? It's because I get a gut feeling. It'll only take five minutes."

"Five minutes?"

"Absolutely."

"I can't miss the fashion show. I make a speech at the end of it."

"Richie, you'll be back. I swear. But don't mention it to anybody. If Elmer finds out, he'll want his picture taken too, and they're just not interested in him. You'll only be gone a couple of minutes."

"Okay. Okay. Sure. Why not? It's kind of fun doing commercials. I can just imagine doing a movie." He hesitated. "The only thing is maybe it's fair for Elmer to have his picture taken too. You know he's always been mad that I got the commercial he was up for."

"Forget Elmer. He's always hanging around the office moaning. See what I mean about not letting this get around? It may not even come off, so keep it under your hat."

Richie put his thumb and forefinger together. Gee-whiz, he thought, maybe this could really turn out to be my lucky day. Somebody might buy my Birdie Panty Hose, and I may become a movie star. The thought should have been reassuring. Instead it made him more nervous as he tapped on the bedroom door.

"Come in," someone yelled. When he opened the door, Annabelle said, "Oh, it's you, Richie. We're all set."

"You girls look great," he said fervently.

They were starting to line up in the order in which they'd appear on the runway. Annabelle was holding a copy of Nora's script. She explained, "Richie, we were doing a run-through," then turned back to the models. "Bessie, when Mrs. Reilly says, 'They come in all colors . . .' "

Richie interrupted, "Girls, I just wanted to wish you luck. I'm gonna ask you to do what I know you're gonna do. Your best. Your very best. For the Fourth Quarter. For home. For country." He swallowed, choked up.

"Get out of here, Richie," Flo ordered. "We know what to do. Bettina," she bellowed, "what's holding you up in there?"

"I must have gotten a sunburn yesterday," a voice called from the bathroom, "all of a sudden my legs itch."

WHEEZING AND GASPING, Ruth raced up the stairwell, threw open the door and stormed down the hallway, her entourage half a flight behind her. This almost makes me want to give up cigarettes, she thought as she aimed for the open door of the manager's penthouse.

Sounds of voices, laughter and music did not reassure her. There was a crowd in there. A crowd of sharks ready to devour the Calla-Lily Company profits, destroy her grandpa's lifework, all because some schlemiel had nothing better to do than invent unsnaggable panty hose.

A horrifying thought hit her. She didn't even know what that schlemiel looked like. She braked long enough to let Barney Freize catch up with her. "What does this jerk look like?" she snarled.

"I'll point him out to you," Barney panted. He knew that Richie might wonder why he was showing up with the people who were trying to buy his patent. Barney didn't care. He didn't trust Ruthy Wuthy as far as you could throw her, which wasn't very far. If she didn't hand over his check at the same minute she tried to get Richie to sign on the dotted line, he'd tell Richie that Ruth wanted his patent at any price.

And she did. But this way, Richie would come out with plenty of big bucks and Barney would have a little nest egg.

They were almost at the door of the suite when Richie stepped into the hallway. "There he is," Barney exclaimed.

In a final burst of speed, Ruth materialized like an apparition in front of Richie. "Five million," she gasped. She waved a paper in front of his face, thrust a pen in his hand. "Sign here. One-time-only offer."

"What?" Richie blinked. From behind he could hear the music fade into the background as Nora began to speak.

"Hello, everyone, and welcome. I'm Nora Regan Reilley, and I'm delighted to have you with us for what I think is one of the most exciting half hours any of you in the panty-hose business will ever experience."

"Sign!" Ruth snarled.

Richie's eyes became unfocused as he saw the check. RICHARD BORIS BLOSSOM . . . FIVE MILLION DOLLARS.

And it was a cashier's check. Not like the ones he and Birdie used to write to each other as a joke on their birthdays. The biggest one they had ever written was for one million dollars. They're kidding, he thought. It's a gag. He spotted Barney.

"Hey, you saved my life last night. What are you trying to do, Barney?" he asked. "Give me a heart attack now? What's this all about?"

He glanced down the hall. Barney was a real card but Richie didn't want to miss the chance to be in a movie.

"It's for real, you dodo," Ruth growled. "And ten percent of the Birdie Panty Hose line of the Calla-Lily Hosiery Company, Inc."

Something hit Richie. This might be on the level. "Wait a minute," he asked, "does your engineer have a mother-in-law who got a manicure yesterday?"

"What the hell does that have to do with anything?" Ruth screamed. "Irving?"

"Yes, Ruthy."

The Calla-Lily contingent was now gathered behind Ruth.

"Did your mother-in-law have her nails done yesterday?" Ruth demanded.

"Yes. And since you ask, she isn't happy about the shade. She thinks it might have a little too much brown in it, Wuthy."

"I'll get you," she hissed between clenched teeth.

This is for real, Richie thought. They've checked out my panty hose. They know it works.

Nora's modulated voice was clear on the loudspeaker. "Our first model is Annabelle. She is wearing a luscious shade of twilight-peach panty hose. Notice how it hugs her legs, how it shimmers in the light, how it flatters the ankle. That's it, Annabelle . . . Let everyone see how beautiful they are . . .'' Ruth heard the genuine applause as the bile rose in her throat.

Down the hall, there was a flurry at the elevator. A bunch of people were getting off.

Ruth looked wild-eyed over her shoulder. Head and shoulders above his entourage and the photographers clustered around him, the familiar face of Dayton Rotter approached like a nightmare come true. Fish or cut bait. That's what Grandpa had always taught her. She forced herself to stand straight, act calm.

"Unless you sign this agreement immediately and accept this check, I officially withdraw my offer," she announced.

With unwilling admiration, Irving thought, Ruthy, I've got to hand it to you. You have guts. He knew if Blossom turned her down, she would kill herself.

Richie wavered. Maybe I'll get more, he thought, his eyes glued on the check. And maybe I won't. Like Ed said, there's nothing you can be sure of except death and taxes. And suppose the other companies like the Birdies a lot but want to take an option till they check them out. That won't buy the Fourth Quarter. This will.

"It's a pleasure to do business with you," he said grandly as he reached for the pen. He started to sign the agreement "Richard Blossom," then hesitated.

Dayton Rotter was footsteps away.

"Sign," Ruth whined.

"Just want to make sure I use my full name so the whole thing is legal," Richie assured her benevolently as, in clear Palmer Method penmanship, he wrote "Richard Boris Blossom."

He put the check in his breast pocket and exchanged a vigorous handshake with Ruth. Still not believing his good fortune, he said, "I never wanted to leave a spot less, but I promised to see someone for just a minute. Why don't you folks go on inside and watch your panty hose being shown off?"

"You bet we will," Ruth gloated as she locked her fingers around the contract. Triumph in her eyes, she smiled viciously as the Rotter entourage entered the foyer and began to watch the fashion show.

"I'll take my check now, too," Barney said to Ruth.

"Give it to him, Ethel," Ruth ordered.

"I have it right here."

ETHEL COULDN'T BELIEVE it. The contract was signed. Now they could all start to breathe again, she hoped. Like Snow White and the Seven Dwarfs, Ruth and the others swept past her to crowd into the room where the fashion show was taking place.

Ethel knew exactly what Ruth was doing. Making up the speech she'd deliver to announce to her rivals that Calla-Lily had struck a deal for Birdie Panty Hose. In a way it was a shame. That panty hose was really pretty and she knew that Ruth wouldn't bring it onto the market until the patent expired. That was in seventeen years. I probably won't be around to get any on discount, Ethel thought.

She realized she needed a couple of aspirins. She'd just take a minute to run down to the suite and get some. Sitting with Ruth since dawn waiting for Preston Landers had been a nerve-racking experience. Ethel thought she'd rather have a full-time job walking pit bulls.

She started down the hall and turned the corner. Mr. Blossom was stepping into the elevator with a tall man. "Hold it, please," she bellowed as she sprinted forward.

Richie smiled benevolently as he held the door, ignoring the photographer who told him to let her wait. "This lady and I just took care of some important business together," he said as Ethel hopped past him into the elevator.

Regan stood nervously in the corner of the room. She didn't want to obstruct anyone's view of the runway. It was going so well she couldn't believe it. She watched the way people were huddling and whispering. She could tell how impressed they were. Even so, it was a long shot that a valid contract could be signed as fast as Richie needed the money.

"It's looking good," Luke whispered in her ear.

Regan glanced up at him. "Dad, where's Richie?"

"He's okay. He's by the door. Said he can't stand to be in here."

"I don't blame him. What the heck was that noise outside?"

"Some latecomers arrived. Over there." He pointed at Ruth and the Calla-Lily group. "Look at the expression on her face. She looks like the cat who ate the canary."

"Never mind them," Regan said. "There's Dayton Rotter. He did get here in time. Keep your fingers crossed."

Six of the models were now clustered beside Nora. Three more were on the runway. They were all in great form, Regan thought. The Fourth Quarter residents were thoroughly in the spirit of the occasion. Bessie lifted her skirt to do a peekaboo of her knee as she coquettishly turned, stopped and posed. Their legs looked great. Regan could see the intense interest on Dayton Rotter's face.

Regan looked over at Nadine, who winked at her as a new CD came on. "Hal-le-lu-jah" started to play. The models near Nora began to sway, building up to the grand finale.

"Rotter missed the beginning," Regan told Luke. "I'm going to talk to him." She slipped through the crowd.

"Stunning!" Regan heard a thin, sharp-featured woman say as she passed. "The whole collection is absolutely stunning."

Dayton Rotter was whispering to Scott, who was shaking his head vigorously. "You've got me wrong," he was saying as Regan approached.

"I don't get things wrong too much," Rotter said. "But I'm sure *you* know who you are. I'm telling you, you're a dead ringer for him."

"Mr. Rotter," Regan began in a low voice. "I'm Regan Reilly. We're so pleased you're able to be here."

Rotter turned from Scott. "I thought I knew this guy," he said in a low voice. "Thought I met him with his uncle in South America last year."

"You didn't," Scott said shortly.

"Well, it wouldn't have been the worst thing if I was right," Rotter told him. "The man I thought was your uncle is one of the few who ever beat me out of a real estate deal."

Regan looked at Scott, who raised his eyebrows and shrugged.

"I've heard a lot about this panty hose," Rotter said quietly. "I'd like to talk to Mr. Blossom afterward."

"That would be wonderful," Regan whispered. "I just wish you had a better view."

"I've got good eyes."

Richie was not standing at the door. He's probably stepped out in the hall, Regan thought. It was almost the finale of the show. He should start moving up toward the microphone to make his speech. I'd better get him.

Before she could take a step toward the door she heard her mother say, "And now Bettina is wearing cameo ivory, the delicate shade that enhances the most enchanting summer frock. Bettina . . . Bettina, we're waiting."

Regan whirled around. Why wasn't Bettina coming out? Someone was obviously signaling. Nora's head was bent. She was looking in the direction of the bedroom.

"Oh, I'm sorry to say that Bettina's extreme case of sunburn has caught up with her. I'm afraid that she can't join us on the runway. So we'll go into our closing number. Ladies . . ."

Regan heard the sound of stifled laughter begin to

ripple through the audience. Bessie was scratching her legs vigorously. Annabelle was poking her to make her stop.

What's the matter with her? Regan wondered. She's ruining the show. And what's the matter with Bettina? Oh, my God, she thought. Is Bessie having an allergic reaction to the panty hose? This would kill Richie. And where the heck was he? She stepped out into the hall. With a sinking feeling she saw that it was empty.

"Bessie," Annabelle whispered. "Cut it out. Everybody's looking at you."

"I can't help it. I feel as though I fell into a patch of poison ivy."

A dismayed Nora heard the whispers around her. "I knew nothing could be that good" was the tone of the remarks. The atmosphere of the room was changing rapidly. People were starting to laugh, many with relief.

Irving leaned forward. The old itch test, he thought. A problem that can pop up no matter how many times you test something. What had brought on the reaction now? He'd bet his bottom dollar that in a few minutes they'd all be clawing themselves. Why is it happening to so many of them at once? He'd have to find out.

"What the hell is going on?" Ruth snarled.

The models were valiantly doing their well-rehearsed version of the Rockettes' famous kick. That only served to give everyone a better view of Bessie's legs, which were now beet-red. But a scream went up in the room when the worst possible disaster of all unfolded. Everyone watched transfixed as a run crept its relentless path up willowy Annabelle's nine-mile legs. "Get him," Ruth shrieked. "Get that lying, cheating schmuck."

She mowed people down as she raced from the room. "Where is he? Where's Blossom?"

ENJOY YOUR PICTURE taking," Ethel said brightly as she left the elevator.

"That is one nice lady," Richie said heartily as the elevator door closed behind her.

Judd Green did not answer.

"I appreciate the chance to try out for the movie. Who did you say the producer is?"

"I didn't. I'm not supposed to say."

Richie's spirits refused to be dampened by the attitude of the man who had introduced himself as the photographer. Richie had protested going downstairs but Green had brusquely explained that his photography equipment was set up in a seminar room off the lobby.

The check in his breast pocket electrified Richie. He was so excited that he hoped he'd be able to concentrate on however they wanted him to pose. He was thinking of the party he had planned to throw if the contract was signed.

"Come on," Judd urged, taking his arm.

Richie hadn't even noticed the elevator had stopped at the lobby. "Oh, sure. Sorry." Dutifully he allowed himself to be hustled from the elevator bank down the deserted hallway to the cluster of abandoned seminar rooms.

The last door was closed. Green knocked on it three times, a staccato rapping.

It was opened instantly. "All set?" Green asked, his voice suddenly genial.

"All set," a burly man in a mover's uniform agreed.

"All set," an equally hefty guy in the same uniform confirmed.

"Holy cow," Richie said as the door closed behind him and he got a look at the room. At least two dozen caskets were lined up. "What is this gonna be, a horror movie?" he asked, laughing.

"You got it," Judd said. "Now we have kind of a funny request for you. You have to climb in this casket for the picture." He indicated one that was open.

"Climb in a casket? Holy smoke. Okay, I've come this far. I thought I was up for a speaking part."

"There's a flashback scene," Judd assured him.

"The crazy things actors will do to get a job," Richie joked as, supported by the two men in uniform, he climbed the little stepladder. " 'Can you jump out of an airplane? Sure. No problem . . . Do you ski with one foot? Every weekend . . . Can you walk a tightrope? Watch me.' ''

He thrust his left leg over the edge. ''Hope I don't get this nice satin lining dirty. Want me to take off my shoes?''

''Just get in.''

Richie obediently hoisted himself into the coffin and asked, ''Sitting up or lying down?''

''Lie down,'' Judd directed. ''Have a smile on your face. I'll take your picture like that. Then, when I say, 'Now,' I want you to sit up straight with a great big grin.''

''It's a comedy, not a horror movie. I like that better,'' Richie confided as he sank his head into the soft ruffles and shut his eyes. ''My wife loved funny movies. She should see me in this one.''

As the coffin lid snapped shut, Richie had the horrifying thought that he hadn't noticed a camera anywhere.

ETHEL TOOK THE elevator back to the penthouse floor. She knew she'd better be there for Ruth's victory speech. Already she was sure the aspirin was doing some good. Her headache was fading. As she turned the corner of the hallway, she ran smack into a young woman.

"Sorry," Regan said, then added quickly, "Are you going to the panty-hose fashion show?"

"Yes." Why on earth did the poor girl look so worried? Ethel wondered.

"Do you by any chance know Richie Blossom?"

"Oh, yes. I just met him."

"Do you know where he is?"

"He went down in the elevator a few minutes ago to have his picture taken."

"His picture taken!" Regan exclaimed. "Where?"

"I'm not sure. Something about a seminar room."

"Was he alone?"

"No. I think the man he was with was a photographer."

Regan experienced a moment of pure despair. "What did that man look like?"

Ethel knew this was serious. She frowned. "Tall," she said quickly. "Thin face. Wearing a light jacket. Wait a minute. When he pressed the elevator button I noticed he had a really mean scrape on the back of his hand."

Oh, my God, Regan thought. With total clarity she could see the hand of the rollerblader scraping along the sidewalk. She raced past Ethel and pressed her finger on the elevator button, holding it there.

Ethel followed her. "Is that nice Mr. Blossom in trouble?"

"Big trouble. My mother is Nora Regan Reilly. Tell her and my father it's an emergency. Send them down to the seminar rooms. They all have to be searched." The elevator door opened. Regan rushed into the car.

Ethel hurried around the corner and flattened herself against the wall as a herd of Calla-Lily directors charged behind Ruth toward the elevator bank. Preston Landers was swinging his lariat, yelling, "This is fun. I never thought I'd say it, but I'm glad to be back."

REGAN RUSHED OFF the elevator and didn't know which way to go. The hallway to the left led to the seminar rooms where the panty-hose convention had been held. She remembered that the funeral convention was down the hallway to the right.

The panty-hose area. That would be a logical place for someone to tell Richie he wanted to take his picture. Not caring that people stared as she passed, she rushed to that section.

The whine of vacuums greeted her. Discarded posters were being bundled into trash cans. There seemed to be an army of maids cleaning up. She could see that all the doors of the rooms were open.

Regan rushed up to a woman with a clipboard who

was supervising the activity. "Is anyone using any of these rooms?" she demanded.

"Nope, they've all cleared out."

"By any chance have you seen two men around here? One is in his seventies, wearing a blue jacket. The other is tall and thin and has a badly scraped hand."

"Haven't seen them." The housekeeper looked pointedly at her clipboard.

Regan turned and raced in the opposite direction. For all she knew, Richie was miles away by now. But she knew he wouldn't leave the building willingly. He had to think his picture was being taken somewhere in here. The woman upstairs who'd been on the elevator with him did say she heard the word "seminar." She'd try the funeral-seminar rooms now. She only prayed that her father had alerted the hotel security to look for Richie.

The moment she reached the corridor of quiet, empty rooms, Regan thought, this is the kind of place Richie might have been taken. She rushed down the hallway, glancing into every room, sweeping her eyes back and forth. Silence. No one.

Her footsteps echoed. The lights were dim in this area, and there were dark shadows along the interior corridor.

She was almost at the end of the hallway. Only one room left. This door was closed. She heard voices inside. She turned the handle. The door was locked.

Something pressed against her back. She whirled her head. Scott was standing behind her. "Need help, Regan?'' he asked as he rapped sharply three times on the door.

Scott! The gasoline can in the garage last night. Dayton Rotter's comments about real estate deals with Scott's uncle. Richie being led off to have his picture taken.

"You!'' Regan breathed. She knew better than to cry out. Scott didn't have to tell her it was the barrel of a gun she was feeling. From inside the room she could hear a thud like a door closing.

Scott rapped again. In that moment, she turned and with all her strength jammed her palm under his nose. His head snapped back and she twisted the gun from his hand. It went off, the bullet hitting the ceiling.

Preston heard the shot as the Calla-Lily group stepped off the elevator. "Enemy fire,'' he howled. Twirling his lariat, he raced past even Ruth, following the direction of the sound.

"Where did you tell my daughter to go?'' Luke asked Ethel urgently.

"I told her that the photographer said something about a seminar room.''

The panty-hose fashion show had come to a tragic end. The special cream Nick had left in his room for them to use on their legs had reacted badly with Richie's new fabric. It had just hit the stores in South Beach a few days before. And if *that* cream could do in the panty hose, others could as well.

The guests were happily ordering more Bloody Marys in unabashed celebration that the threat to their business had been permanently snagged.

Nadine had just received a request for a replay of "Hal-le-lujah" from H. Mason Hicks, Junior, a beaming panty-hose executive.

"Drop dead," she told him.

Nick hurried over to Luke. "What else is wrong?"

On his way out the door, Nora at his side, Luke stopped long enough to snap, "We think Richie's in trouble and Regan is trying to find him."

"I'll put out an alert."

"She was going to the seminar rooms first," Ethel cried as she ran behind Luke and Nora.

"Something's up, Nadine," Joey said.

From across the room Nadine had seen the distress in Luke's face. "Let's go find out, Joey," she said.

RICHIE TRIED TO bang his arms against the lid of the casket. The thick satin lining muffled the sound. He felt the casket being wheeled and heard a door opening. Those guys weren't actors, he thought. He tried to shout and knew that it was no use.

The casket was picked up, bumped into the side of something, then Richie felt himself being slid, as if they were pushing the casket into a van. Oh, Birdie, he thought, what do I do now?

Take it easy, he thought. Breathe slowly. There can't be much air in this thing.

He heard the sound of an engine, then whatever vehicle he was in began to move.

* * *

Regan aimed the gun at Scott. Someone must have heard the shot, she thought frantically. There was no longer any sound inside the room. This had to be where they'd taken Richie. What were they doing to him?

Scott was trying to come nearer. Wiping the blood from his nose, edging toward her, his eyes calculating.

"Don't take another step," she said.

"You wouldn't shoot me, Regan." His hand shot up; he lunged toward her. She aimed the gun down at his foot. She'd stop him if she had to.

An ear-splitting whoop made Scott jump.

"Need any help, ma'am?" Preston Landers hollered, hurling his lasso, which to Regan's astonishment settled around Scott's shoulders. "Want me to hog-tie this pup? My posse's on the way."

Regan was frantic to find Richie. She saw the crowd of people approaching. "This man is dangerous, hold on to him," she called.

Irving was a step behind Ruth. "We'll take care of him."

"Where's Blossom?" Ruth screamed.

Regan tried to open the door. It was locked.

"Stand aside, everybody," she commanded. "I've got to fire this gun to get the door open."

With the exception of Ruth, they scattered like leaves in the wind. Preston held one end of the rope as Irving herded the lassoed Scott into a nearby room.

Regan took aim. One bullet was enough to shatter the lock. She rushed into the room and gasped as she saw the rows of coffins. The room was completely still. She raced for the door at the far end of the room.

As she shoved it open, she saw a nondescript van pulling away. Taking aim, she fired at the back tires.

From behind her she could hear shouting voices—her father's, Nick's, Joey's.

Her first shot had barely missed the farther rear tire. Steadying the gun on her left wrist, she aimed again. This time she was rewarded by the sound of a blowout. The van careened. Once again she aimed. Got you, she thought as the other back tire blew. If only I'm not too late.

Three men jumped from the van. Luke, Joey and Nick appeared from behind Regan and began to chase them.

"Be careful," Regan shouted. "They may be armed."

Nick caught up with the tallest and jumped on his back, tackling him to the ground as security guards poured into the area and subdued the other two.

Regan raced to the van and yanked open the doors. The coffin. Richie had to be in it. She jumped up, crouched beside it, fumbled, desperate to open the lid.

She hear the click as the lock released, uttered a fervent prayer and raised the lid. A pale Richie smiled up at her. "Boy, are you a sight for sore eyes!" he said.

"Oh, Richie, I'm so glad you're all right," Regan said.

"So how'd the show go?" he asked.

"Richie, I have bad news. There is something wrong with the panty hose after all. You won't be able to sell it."

"You're right, Regan, I won't." Richie reached in

his breast pocket and pulled out the cashier's check for five million dollars. "I already did. Let's get to one of the quick-deposit machines."

Ruth was trying to climb into the van. "Thief. Impostor. Liar. Cheat. Scoundrel."

Richie whispered. "Regan, quick, put the lid down."

A CHEER WENT up in the Dolly Twiggs Memorial Room Monday afternoon as Richie ceremoniously received the deed for the Fourth Quarter from Dolly's sister, Lucille. A delighted Joey represented the real estate agency in the transaction.

"Speaking for my sister, Dolly, I am thrilled that you will all be able to stay in the house that she so loved," Lucille gushed. She was so happy she almost couldn't speak. Arthur had surprised her by flying in that morning. "I love Lucy," he'd said, "and I missed her more every day. I couldn't wait any longer to see her." Lucille gazed at him across the room. He winked back at her and threw a kiss.

"Thank you, Lucille. Bless your memory, Dolly.

Long live the residents of this home," Richie declared. "For it is ours and ours forever."

Flo put down her tray of Gatorade and cookies to lead the vigorous applause.

"And now, everybody," Richie concluded, "the caterers should be ready for us out back. They've got champagne and anything you can think of to eat. Enjoy."

He stepped from the podium and hugged a beaming Ethel. She was so special. And she'd played a part in his rescue by telling Regan where he'd disappeared to.

"I feel a little guilty about Ruth," he whispered to her, but looking into Ethel's smiling eyes made him forget. It was almost like when he had looked at Birdie.

"Don't feel guilty, Richie. They have her in therapy now." Ethel and Richie both laughed.

"You're bad," he said. "I love it."

"Richie."

Richie turned and Elaine was standing there. "From now on," she said, "I'm the only one who sends you on auditions, okay?"

"Okay, boss."

"Of course now I've got to hire a replacement for that ne'er-do-well."

"I'm available," Ethel piped up. "Believe me, I'm available."

Barney Freize came up and shook Richie's hand. "I've got to hand it to you, Richie. I was thinking that I wouldn't mind getting an apartment in this place. That is, if you're allowed to smoke cigars!"

"We'd love to have you living here, Barney. We'd

light up out on the front porch and watch the world go by.'' Richie looked around the room and got a lump in his throat. He was with all his friends. Everyone looked so happy. Even Elmer.

Regan leaned against the back wall and smiled. All's well that ends well, she thought. When Scott had been promised that the prosecutor wouldn't press for the death penalty if he came clean, he'd sung his heart out. His uncle had quietly bought up the property adjacent to the Fourth Quarter and had wanted to build a luxury resort building, which would have included space for a modeling agency for Scott. Judd Green was their hit man. Scott admitted that Green had been paid to kill Dolly last year. Elmer had unwittingly kept Scott abreast of the Fourth Quarter's attempts to raise money to save their home. They hadn't worried about the pot-holder sales, but when Elmer started talking about Richie's snag-proof panty hose, they got nervous and thought they might not get to buy the Fourth Quarter.

Nick was nearby holding the hand of one of the models who'd fallen in love when she'd witnessed his bravery on Saturday. They followed Luke and Nora and Ed and Bridget out to where the party was starting.

John and Maura were standing next to Regan. Their luggage was in the car. Everyone had had a great time at their wedding yesterday and had partied at the hotel until the wee hours.

"We couldn't miss this," Maura said to Regan. "We're going to grab a glass of that champagne and be off."

"I think our parents are back there popping the cor
right now," Regan laughed.

Nadine and Joey came over to Regan.

"You know, Regan, now that Scott's in the poke
I'm going to need a new roommate," Joey said a
paused. "I asked Nadine to marry me."

"What a Romeo," Nadine beamed. "And I want
ask you, Regan, if you'll put on another one of tho
awful dresses in a few months and be a bridesmaid f
me."

"I'd love to. Let's get a drink so we can toast you

They started out the door when Richie called Regan
name. Regan turned and found him standing in front
her with Ethel at his side. There was a flicker in his ey
she hadn't seen for a long time.

"I'm so proud of you, Richie," Regan said.

"Proud of me? You're the one who saved my life
don't know how to repay you. But what I was thinki
of doing was dedicating this new invention I'm worki
on to you . . ." He put one arm around Regan, the oth
around Ethel as he led them to the back patio of t
Fourth Quarter. "What I did was take this little gizn
and fiddle around with it and before you knew it . .

About the Author

Carol Higgins Clark is the author of ten best-selling Regan Reilly mysteries. DECKED was nominated for both an Anthony and an Agatha Award for best first novel. Carol is co-author, along with her mother, Mary Higgins Clark, of four best-selling holiday mysteries. Also an actress, Carol studied at the Beverly Hills Playhouse and has recorded several of her mother's works as well as her own novels. She received an AudioFile's Earphones Award of Excellence for her reading of JINXED. She is a graduate of Mount Holyoke College and lives in New York City. Visit her Web site at www.carolhigginsclark.com.